It was a desperate plan that required perfect timing

The Land Rover lurched forward an inch and Bolan pressed harder on the brake pedal, his muscles cramping under the strain. Drops of stinging sweat trickled into his eyes as he waited patiently for his enemies. Despite the agony that screamed from within his arm and shoulder, he willed himself to push harder.

The SUV suddenly appeared, coming fast around the curve. A split second later it was in front of the grotto, its engine racing against the elevation. Bolan released the brake and fell back as his vehicle surged forward, smashing into the SUV's passenger side.

Shrieks of twisting metal and screaming tires filled the air.

The two vehicles plunged over the edge of the cliff, falling through the air for three or four long seconds before crashing onto the rocks below. There was a brief silence before both cars exploded, sending sound waves that merged and echoed as one across the Irish countryside.

Bolan rose from his position and peered over the edge. He had won this particular battle—but the Executioner had no doubt that this war was just beginning.

MACK BOLAN®
The Executioner

#270 Judgment Day
#271 Cyberhunt
#272 Stealth Striker
#273 UForce
#274 Rogue Target
#275 Crossed Borders
#276 Leviathan
#277 Dirty Mission
#278 Triple Reverse
#279 Fire Wind
#280 Fear Rally
#281 Blood Stone
#282 Jungle Conflict
#283 Ring of Retaliation
#284 Devil's Army
#285 Final Strike
#286 Armageddon Exit
#287 Rogue Warrior
#288 Arctic Blast
#289 Vendetta Force
#290 Pursued
#291 Blood Trade
#292 Savage Game
#293 Death Merchants
#294 Scorpion Rising
#295 Hostile Alliance
#296 Nuclear Game
#297 Deadly Pursuit
#298 Final Play
#299 Dangerous Encounter
#300 Warrior's Requiem
#301 Blast Radius
#302 Shadow Search
#303 Sea of Terror
#304 Soviet Specter
#305 Point Position
#306 Mercy Mission
#307 Hard Pursuit
#308 Into the Fire
#309 Flames of Fury
#310 Killing Heat
#311 Night of the Knives
#312 Death Gamble
#313 Lockdown
#314 Lethal Payload
#315 Agent of Peril
#316 Poison Justice
#317 Hour of Judgment
#318 Code of Resistance
#319 Entry Point
#320 Exit Code
#321 Suicide Highway
#322 Time Bomb
#323 Soft Target
#324 Terminal Zone
#325 Edge of Hell
#326 Blood Tide
#327 Serpent's Lair
#328 Triangle of Terror
#329 Hostile Crossing
#330 Dual Action
#331 Assault Force
#332 Slaughter House
#333 Aftershock
#334 Jungle Justice
#335 Blood Vector
#336 Homeland Terror
#337 Tropic Blast
#338 Nuclear Reaction
#339 Deadly Contact
#340 Splinter Cell
#341 Rebel Force
#342 Double Play
#343 Border War
#344 Primal Law
#345 Orange Alert

The Don Pendleton's

Executioner®

ORANGE ALERT

TORONTO • NEW YORK • LONDON
AMSTERDAM • PARIS • SYDNEY • HAMBURG
STOCKHOLM • ATHENS • TOKYO • MILAN
MADRID • WARSAW • BUDAPEST • AUCKLAND

First edition August 2007

ISBN-13: 978-0-373-64345-5
ISBN-10: 0-373-64345-4

Special thanks and acknowledgment to
Peter Spring for his contribution to this work.

ORANGE ALERT

Printed in U.S.A.

Peace is produced by war.

—Latin Proverb

I continue my fight in order to preserve peace.

—Mack Bolan

THE MACK BOLAN LEGEND

Nothing less than a war could have fashioned the destiny of the man called Mack Bolan. Bolan earned the Executioner title in the jungle hell of Vietnam.

But this soldier also wore another name—Sergeant Mercy. He was so tagged because of the compassion he showed to wounded comrades-in-arms and Vietnamese civilians.

Mack Bolan's second tour of duty ended prematurely when he was given emergency leave to return home and bury his family, victims of the Mob. Then he declared a one-man war against the Mafia.

He confronted the Families head-on from coast to coast, and soon a hope of victory began to appear. But Bolan had broken society's every rule. That same society started gunning for this elusive warrior—to no avail.

So Bolan was offered amnesty to work within the system against terrorism. This time, as an employee of Uncle Sam, Bolan became Colonel John Phoenix. With a command center at Stony Man Farm in Virginia, he and his new allies—Able Team and Phoenix Force—waged relentless war on a new adversary: the KGB.

But when his one true love, April Rose, died at the hands of the Soviet terror machine, Bolan severed all ties with Establishment authority.

Now, after a lengthy lone-wolf struggle and much soul-searching, the Executioner has agreed to enter an "arm's-length" alliance with his government once more, reserving the right to pursue personal missions in his Everlasting War.

Prologue

A cloud passed in front of the moon, and the moors became so dark Steven Oxford couldn't even see his hand in front of his face, much less the outlines of the three men who stood in the ankle-high grass with him. The wind picked up from the east, gusting across Lake Erne, carrying with it the earthy scent of peat and a chill that penetrated Oxford's heavy black wool sweater and the long-sleeved cotton T-shirt he wore underneath. Even in July, the moors between Donegal Bay and the lakes became uncomfortably cold at night.

In a belt holster tucked into the small of his back, Oxford carried a Glock 17, the standard handgun issued to CIA operatives.

A few months earlier, during his annual requalification, Oxford had placed ten of the seventeen 9 mm rounds into a two-and-a-half-inch circle at twenty-five yards—exactly twice the quantity required. Oxford was a man who liked to keep track of those details even more than the CIA did. His office walls at Langley were covered with citations and certifications, all arranged in precise chronological order.

The cloud passed, exposing the moon's thin crescent, enabling the outlines of the waiting men to become discernable as blobs of deeper darkness against the sepia blanket that cloaked the moors. Oxford's three companions were also dressed in black, their features highlighted by the silvery illumination, giving the impression that their faces floated like decapitated heads in ghostly search of their lost bodies.

A freight train rumbled in the distance, one of many that traveled the railroad tracks crisscrossing the moors. Barely audible above the clack and clatter of the passing train was the howl of a dog—a mournful sound that echoed over the wasteland to be answered a few seconds later by another of its species. Had Oxford been superstitious, the wail would have sent a shiver down his spine. But neither *superstition* nor *fear* were words in the agent's vocabulary. Despite standing on a moor in the middle of the night in an Irish county where half the population over sixty years of age swore to personal knowledge of banshees, he was confident that he and the Glock could handle whatever came their way.

He took a swift, visual inventory of his companions. Bobbie Reegan was clearly the most dangerous, driven by a hate so fiery his eyes sometimes glowed as if lit from behind. The other two were no more than common thugs, losers drawn to the Orange Order in much the same way that Oxford thought skinheads were attracted to organizations spewing white supremacy. Political motives, if considered at all, were secondary. Blacks, Catholics, Jews, it didn't matter whose blood they were spilling—it was the actual hate and killing that pulled them in.

The night's meeting with Cypher would be an important one. He'd said they'd be assigned their targets and given half the money, which meant that Oxford's undercover assignment was coming to an end. Once Cypher doled out the actual missions, it was Oxford's time to fish or cut bait, to convey all the intel to his superiors and move on.

Oxford felt, rather than saw or heard, Cypher's arrival. There was a slight compression of air, and he and his sidekick were suddenly in their midst.

As they had for the previous three meets, Cypher and his companion wore ski masks that covered everything but their eyes and mouths, making them look not ghostly, but more like the Cheshire cat.

Oxford turned his full attention to the new arrivals. Even the extreme darkness could not hide the physical bulk of the man who accompanied Cypher. His widely spaced eyes and mouth floated a good six inches above everyone else's, and the patch of deeper darkness representing his body's volume was twice that of Reegan's. Oxford recalled that at the group's very first meeting, the man had moved his muscular frame in a threatening manner that told everyone he was no stranger to the martial arts. This guy, Oxford thought again while tapping his molars together as if the chilly air was making him shiver, was obviously a bodyguard.

Cypher came immediately to the point, speaking in a rustling voice reminiscent of leaves being blown across a brick courtyard in winter.

"The committee has chosen targets. Randolph's cell is first," he said, as if everyone in Ireland was privy to the classified knowledge that Peter Randolph was head of a special group of CIA operatives whose mission was to coordinate the defection of former Soviet scientists.

Randolph's cell? The words took Oxford by surprise.

Although the splinter group had been formed a short three months earlier with the four members supposedly being handpicked by Cypher himself, Oxford had infiltrated the Orange Order more than a year before, and there had never been any talk of directing violence against anyone except the Catholics. What was driving this shift in tactics? he wondered.

"Reegan," Cypher stated, "you'll be the one to hit Randolph. He's on holiday now, but he'll be back at his home base in Stuttgart starting next week, and we're thinking that will be the best place to do it. We'll give you everything you need."

Reegan grunted his understanding.

Accompanied by the crinkling sound of paper, Cypher said, "Here's an envelope with half your money. You'll get the rest when you do the job."

Oxford heard Reegan stuff the payment into his pants pocket. He was amazed at what Cypher was saying. Not only were these guys planning to hit the CIA, they apparently had access to company information. Randolph's supervisor should have been the only person to know when one of his active operatives was taking vacation. Was there a leak in security? And if there was, how far up the chain did it go?

Oxford tapped his molars together while contemplating the impact of Cypher's words. If the plan was to kill everyone in the cell, he had to warn Randolph about the three operatives he knew were carried on his roster.

"Taylor, Buckley and Johnston will also be hit this week."

Oxford heard Cypher say their names as a strong arm suddenly clasped him from behind, and in one swift move snatched the Glock from his belt holster. Too late, he realized, he had failed to notice Cypher's bodyguard slipping behind him. He pushed with all his might, attempting to expand his shoulders to open enough space for an elbow jab, but the arm around him was like an iron vise.

The huge man squeezed, and Oxford's breath was driven from his lungs. He saw stars and thought for a moment he was blacking out, but the moment passed, and he drew a shallow breath that kept him conscious.

"There's a traitor in our group," Cypher said in a dry voice.

There were two poisonous darts in Oxford's wristwatch, each loaded with a derivative of venom produced by central eastern Australia's inland taipan, the most lethal viper in the world. Scientists at the CIA had refined the toxin, creating a poison hundreds of times more deadly. The result was a substance powerful enough to bestow upon a tiny dart the capability to deliver almost immediate death.

Held as he was, Oxford was unable to reach the watch's trigger button with his right hand. His mind racing, he realized that, if he could knock his shoes together, the blade inside his right heel would snap into place, and he'd be able to stab his captor's shin.

Like a movie viewed in fast forward, the scenario flashed through the agent's mind. Reacting to the unexpected stab to his leg, the bodyguard would release him and, in less than two seconds, both he and Cypher would feel the prick of death stored inside the wristwatch. Oxford could quickly dispatch the other three, barehanded if necessary.

As if the huge man could read his thoughts, Oxford was suddenly thrown forward into the darkness. He landed on his knees, spinning immediately upon hitting the ground while reaching for his left wrist.

Excruciating pain, the likes of which he had never exprienced, shot through Oxford's arm and into his brain as a 9 mm round from his own weapon smashed into the watch and continued through his wrist, leaving his hand dangling by a few bloody tendons. Ever the professional, the first impression to register in his mind above the searing agony was that the bodyguard must have slipped on night goggles to make such a shot.

His second thought, coming nanoseconds after the first, was to get the hell out of there.

Oxford lunged and took two quick steps before a round caught him in the back of the knee, blowing his patella onto the ground before him in a shower of bone chips and blood. He pitched forward, writhing in pain so intense that he lost awareness of all other sensations. The cold ground rushed up as he slammed onto his face, breathing raggedly, inhaling small bits of dirt laced with a peaty residue that tasted of decay.

A heavy boot smashed into his side, taking his breath away and flipping him onto his back. Oxford fought hard to keep from passing out. He knew he was about to die, and he wanted to be fully aware when it happened, facing death head-on, the way a warrior would.

Cypher's bodyguard loomed over him. High above the Irish countryside, the sliver of the moon shimmered, illuminating the short barrel of Oxford's Glock as the cold steel was pressed against his forehead.

In the distance, an animal wailed. Cypher said, "We'll see who comes for him," and there was a brilliant flash of white light that ended the CIA agent's life.

Mack Bolan listened to the rhythmic signal coming through his earpiece. The cadence was strong and steady. As he got closer the beat would get faster and, during his final one hundred yards, the pitch would change if he veered off course. Judging from the spacing between notes, Bolan knew his objective was a ways off, maybe as far as three miles.

When the GPS finally led him to within one yard of the tiny transmitter implanted inside agent Oxford's molar, Bolan's earpiece would begin to hum a steady tone.

As he listened to the steady electronic pulse, the soldier was confident that the system would lead him directly to his goal.

In keeping with his practice for night missions, Bolan's six-foot-three-inch frame was dressed entirely in black, from his jump boots that trod silently across the hard ground of the moors, to the knitted wool hat that covered his closely cut hair. The green-black-and-brown jungle camouflage he had smeared on the high points of his hawkish features absorbed the silvery sheen of moonlight, rendering him invisible against the dark countryside.

On his hip he wore a .44-caliber Desert Eagle and, in the pouches attached to the web belt, he carried, among other items, several clips of ammunition.

A holster on his left shoulder held a 9 mm Beretta 93-R, and a foot-long Fairbairn-Sykes combat knife rested in a weathered black leather sheath strapped to the outside of his right calf.

The man some called the Executioner didn't know if he would actually need the weapons he carried, but he had been walking the hellfire trail too long to approach any mission unrepared. Despite the tranquil appearance the Irish countryside offered, a CIA agent had lost his life three nights earlier, and, to Bolan, that made the area a combat zone. More than once, Bolan had seen supposedly cold spots turn unexpectedly hot in seconds. He hadn't survived all these years by being careless. Parking his rental car more than two miles away and coming in on foot was only the first precaution.

The Irish coast near the Ulster border was rugged country, with narrow, winding roads twisting through bowl-shaped contours of land extending from Lake Erne to Donegal Bay. In the daylight, views, at times, were nothing short of spectacular as the trails meandering through barren moors suddenly emerged upon sheep-studded pastures, so intensely green they were almost blinding. Immediately south of the moors, where Bolan had parked his car under the cover of a thin stand of hickory trees, the way became treacherous, perilously clinging to the sides of cliffs rising straight up from the sea where, hundreds of feet below, angry surf pounded the craggy coastline. Small religious shrines were carved at irregular intervals into the side of the rock walls to commemorate locations where fugitive priests had celebrated Mass during the British repression.

The trouble here had started, as so many conflicts in the history of man have, over religion. Protestant against Catholic, both sides killing for Christ, with the escalating violence over a period of more than two generations spawning the Orange Order, the IRA and twenty or thirty splinter groups, each with its own vision of tomorrow's Ireland. For the most part, the rest of the world had ignored the conflict. A bunch of Irishmen killing each other on their tiny island way up in the North Atlantic didn't threaten world stability the way an outbreak of war in the oil rich Middle East would.

Under normal circumstances, a man like Mack Bolan wouldn't have been the one called into Ireland for a CIA find-and-retrieve mission, but the communiqué had been sent straight up the chain of command to the director of Homeland Security, who'd immediately alerted the President of its contents. The chief executive had decided he wanted someone with no traceable ties to a government agency, The call had gone out on a secured line to Hal Brognola at the Justice Department.

"They have to take it seriously," Brognola had said later that day when he'd met Bolan on the National Mall in the shadow of the Museum of Natural History. They'd been walking west along Madison Drive, the domed Capitol building at their backs gleaming a brilliant white in the light from the afternoon sun.

The big Fed had continued. "This is much more than just an agent getting murdered, Striker. A terrorist group threatening to assassinate cabinet members? Jesus. The President wants someone to help assess how credible these people are."

Brognola was fully aware of the Bolan's arm's-length relationship with the government, but he also knew that the soldier had never refused a request from his old friend. Brognola's agenda usually was in tune with the Executioner's. But Bolan would decide on his own whether or not to accept the mission.

Bolan had remained silent, studying the transcript he'd been reading as they'd walked.

"What's this about another 9/11?" he asked.

"That's the part that has the President most concerned," Brognola answered. "The CIA doesn't need any help dealing with these guys if they're just a bunch of crackpots trying to make a statement. But, if what we're up against is an organized terrorist cell with the capability to carry out those threats, we have to know who they are, and we have to know it now. All the President wants you to do is to get the CIA pointed in the right direction."

It had been the part about another September 11 that had convinced Bolan to take the assignment.

He had met with Edmund Fontes, the director of CIA activities in Ireland, who'd reluctantly given him Steven Oxford's final field report. In it, the late agent had described Cypher and the terrorist cell the mysterious man was forming, but there was no mention of any targets other than Catholic organizations in Ireland.

"He was one of my best," Fontes had said tersely while handing Bolan the report, "and, if it was up to me, we'd go in and get him, ourselves. This is our job, and we don't like someone else doing it."

Bolan took no umbrage at the CIA man's resentment. The way he received missions all but guaranteed that he'd be treading on someone else's turf from the minute he showed up. He'd go in, get the microchip for Brognola, the one Oxford had in a back molar, and see what developed from there.

Now, twenty-four hours after saying he'd take the assignment, he was on-site, closing in on his objective.

An animal howled in the distance, and Bolan paused to take his bearings. Close by, a freight train rumbled over tracks on its way to the industrialized areas to the north.

The homing signal's beat suddenly picked up, and Bolan's senses went on full alert. With the terrain's undulating dips and swells dotted with sparse patches of tall bushes and wind-blown hickory trees, the area was perfect for an ambush.

Bolan walked quickly, his eyes scanning the darkness, his free ear processing a steady flow of sounds. Noise carried well over the moors. Not as well as over water, where the crack of a gunshot could carry for miles.

He heard them before they were aware of his presence. A metallic click lasting no more than a millisecond rode to his ears on the night's currents. It might have been the sound of a buckle that hadn't been taped, or a snap fastening someone's top collar against the breeze, but to a soldier with Bolan's honed senses, it just as well could have been a bullhorn announcing their location.

Dropping to one knee, he reached into the pouch on his web belt containing his night-vision goggles. As he adjusted the goggles on his face, Bolan turned off his earpiece. He'd deal with the ambush first, then locate Oxford. From the signal he had been getting and the direction he thought the errant sound came from, his greeting party appeared to be positioned close to his objective.

Bolan focused the goggles, bringing the moors into sharp relief. There was a flurry of movement off to his left as a pair of jackrabbits dodged and sprinted their way through the underbrush. He scanned from left to right, pausing at every patch of bushes and trees, watching for unnatural movement. A halo of light flared briefly, the flame of a cigarette lighter magnified tens of thousands of times as its photons passed through the photocathode tube of his goggles.

Amateurs, Bolan thought. *Undisciplined, untrained amateurs.*

He switched the goggles to infrared mode, and the scene before him shimmered slightly as he painted the landscape with IR. Three men were positioned in a clump of trees about a hundred yards off to his right, their figures clear and distinct against the cooler foliage. A slight spiral extended upward from the man who was smoking, his cigarette heating the air directly above him.

Bolan removed the goggles and returned them to their pouch. The men waiting for him obviously knew that Oxford was wearing a transmitter that would lead someone to his remains. Did they also know that he had been a CIA plant? And, if they did, what were their intentions now for the man who came to retrieve him?

Regardless of what they had been planning, the Executioner thought they were about to get more than they'd bargained for.

He rose into a crouch and set off, as silent as an owl swooping from above to snatch unsuspecting prey. When he finally got to a point about twenty yards behind them and they became visible in the dim light, he lowered himself again to one knee and took note of how the three were set up. He figured they would be facing his objective. He switched the earpiece back on.

The beat was coming in as an almost steady tone, and the note had changed, indicating Bolan was slightly off center. Before turning the signal off, he mentally extrapolated the sound with his position and that of the ambush, arriving at a spot about fifty yards from where he thought Oxford's body would be buried.

He withdrew a powerful penlight from his front shirt pocket and rotated the lens to produce a beam. Sliding the Desert Eagle from its holster, he stood and took a step forward.

"Everyone freeze!" he shouted in a voice full of authority as he held it out at a full arm's length to the left of his body.

The three men, suddenly illuminated, simultaneously

made the wrong decision. As the two men flanking the third threw themselves to the ground, the man in the middle turned and fired a pistol, the round snapping the air directly beneath Bolan's penlight, which he switched off while lunging to his right. In midair, he squeezed the Desert Eagle's trigger once, and the throaty roar of the weapon delivered instant death to his attacker as the heavy round slammed through the man's chest, exiting through his back in a messy hole the size of a heavyweight's fist.

Bolan rolled quickly as bullets from the other two gunmen sliced the air where he had been a split second earlier. Using one of the muzzle-flashes for a target, Bolan fired two shots so close together that they echoed across the moors as a single retort. He immediately heard the heavy thump of a body being hammered into hard earth, and all was still.

Continuing his roll to the right, Bolan strained his ears for the sound of his enemy's breathing. In the sudden silence, he could hear it—raspy and quick. The man was off to his left, about ten yards away, and apparently still standing upright.

Bolan considered taking him alive in order to gain some intel about the communiqué. Before he could initiate his next move, however, panic apparently got the better of his adversary, who abruptly let loose with a barrage of automatic pistol fire aimed a full four feet above Bolan. With the shooter illuminated by his series of quick muzzle-blasts, Bolan zeroed in from his prone position and fired once, drilling a hole through the man's gut. The force of the Eagle's .44-caliber punch threw the hardman four feet and he crumpled into a lifeless heap, oozing intestines that shimmered and shone black in the intermittent moonlight.

Like most firefights, this one had been quick and violent.

The acrid smell of cordite hung heavy in the air, mingling with the fresh stink of death that filled Bolan's nostrils. He remained in his prone position, listening intently for any sound of life. After a good thirty seconds, he rose to his full height. Holding the penlight out to his left again, he switched it on.

All three men were dead.

Bolan quickly scanned the area, anxious to complete his mission. There was no vehicle, which meant that these men had either left their means of transportation somewhere and walked to the site as Bolan had, or they had been dropped off by other team members who were still very much alive.

In the beam of his penlight, tire tracks were visible in the dirt, confirming Bolan's worst-case hunch. He rushed forward to check the bodies, intent on removing any identification they might be carrying. As he patted down the first corpse, he noticed the gleam of a silver chain around the man's neck. With the same motion he had used more often than he wanted to remember when pulling the dog tags from a fallen comrade, Bolan snapped the chain free and stuffed it into his pants pocket. He continued checking the body for identification, and, finding none, moved on to the other two with the same results. None carried ID of any kind, but all three had worn a medal around their necks.

Turning his back to the bodies, Bolan switched his earpiece receiver back on. The signal was strong and steady, and as he sprinted to the spot he had selected before the firefight broke out, the tone became solid. In the moonlight, Bolan could see the dim outline that had the correct dimensions for a shallow grave. When he stood over it, the earpiece told him he had found his mark.

He pulled the foot-long combat knife from its sheath and plunged it into the soft earth. Just as the hilt touched ground, the tip of the blade made contact. In the distance, Bolan could hear a new sound—the steady drone of a vehicle that sounded big. He didn't know for sure how distant it was, but the way sound traveled over the moors, he thought he had at least five minutes before it would reach him. He began to claw at the grave, moving the loose soil to both sides. In less than a minute, he reached the body. Holding the penlight with his teeth, he saw that luck was with him—the end he had chosen to clear exposed Oxford's head, the upper portion above the agent's eyebrows mangled and singed around the edges by the point-blank shot that had taken his life. The bottom half of his face was smeared with dirt and, after three days in the grave, swollen beyond recognition.

Leaning forward, Bolan grabbed the corpse's head and brushed the dirt away from its mouth. Placing the point of his combat knife at a spot directly beneath Oxford's earlobe, he opened the agent's cheek with a quick forward slice, revealing teeth that shone like pearls in the penlight's beam. In the back of the dead man's throat, insects scurried to escape the sudden illumination.

Bolan pushed the flap of bloodless skin away so he could insert the tip of his blade under the last molar. In the back of his mind, he was aware that the vehicle was drawing closer, coming slowly due to the winding roads, but approaching, nevertheless, at a steady pace. As he twisted the knife's handle and the dead agent's tooth popped free, Bolan wondered what had prompted its approach. Whether it was responding to the sound of gunfire traveling a great distance through the clear still night, or a missed call-in from the men waiting in ambush, the result was the same—there was no time to retrieve Oxford's remains. But Bolan had the most important thing he had come for and he could mark the body's location for a future pickup by placing his earpiece with the corpse.

He dropped the extracted molar into the same pocket containing the chains he had taken from his would-be ambushers, shoved his earpiece down the front of Oxford's blood-enrusted sweater and hurriedly pushed the dirt back over the body. Just as he was finishing, he caught the glimpse of approaching headlights winding their way down the side of the shallow bowl-shaped valley less than a quarter of a mile away.

After smoothing the earth back over the shallow grave, he ran at full speed for a stand of trees and thick bushes about a hundred yards away. He had progressed less than ten feet into the woods when an SUV burst out of the adjacent hillside pasture onto the flat land of the moors, and the night was suddenly filled with the eardrum-splitting sounds of AK-47s chattering in full-automatic mode.

The air surrounding Bolan became a deadly beehive of activity as bullets whizzed by with the distinctive snaps of 7.62 mm bullets. He dived to the ground, scrambling for cover.

The furious fusillade ended abruptly, and Bolan heard the distinctive metallic rattling of empty magazines being ejected, followed by the slide and click of new ones being rammed home. In the sudden silence, rendered more profound by its extreme contrast to the deafening uproar from the AK-47s that still echoed in his brain, a wide beam of blinding light painted the trees and thick bushes with broad strokes, sweeping back and forth through the stretch of woods like a prison spotlight.

From his prone position in a tiny depression behind a stout hickory, Bolan flexed his legs in preparation for his departure. He peered through the lush foliage, inches above ground level, to where the SUV stood like an alien being, its modern technology seeming anachronistic against the barren landscape.

Accompanied by the racing sound of its powerful engine, the vehicle spun in a cloud of dust, casting its lights onto the ambush site littered with three bodies. As Bolan moved in a crouch through the woods to put distance between himself and the new arrivals, he heard the opening of a door followed by loud cursing in a thick brogue. A quick burst of automatic fire sliced through the trees at least fifty yards to his left. It was an obvious gesture of anger and frustration, and it reinforced Bolan's earlier opinion that his opponents were deficient in both their training and discipline. This lack of professionalism would be a factor he'd leverage to his advantage when they finally clashed again, which was bound to happen sooner or later.

The SUV wasn't able to follow him through the trees, but Bolan knew that the stand would eventually end and he'd find himself at the edge of a sheep pasture somewhere with no available cover. If the men in the vehicle were locals, they'd know the place where the woods ended, and that's where they'd be waiting.

Crouching behind a thick tree, Bolan checked his watch for the time: 2:30 a.m. The summer equinox had occurred a scant two weeks earlier, which meant that, at this time of year, sunrise came quickly to the regions up around the fifty-fifth parallel. The area was at about the same latitude as Glasgow, where dawn would break around four-thirty. Bolan didn't know how long it would take him to reach the tracks where he'd heard the trains rumbling, but he thought it would be to his advantage to get there before daybreak.

As he made his way through the woods, Bolan recalled the information contained in the second communiqué that had been delivered to the local CIA office and forwarded to the President. The Apprentices, a rogue splinter group claiming to be sponsored by the Orange Order, was demanding immediate disarmament of the IRA, and international recognition for the legitimacy of home rule in Belfast. Once and for all, they wanted the world—and especially the United States—to endorse the existence of two nations in Ireland and to formally declare that there was no chance the two would ever be united. Once and for all, they wanted to end the Irish conflict, and they were prepared to use terrorism to force the result.

They further said they were about to release a list of prominent Catholics, whose assassinations were being scheduled to occur until the process of IRA disarmament was complete. And, finally, they were threatening the United States with a domestic terrorist attack if their demands were not met by the end of July. That gave the CIA less than a month to find and destroy the people behind the plot.

It was an insane scenario, made viable by the global terrorism that had spread like a runaway cancer since the fateful assault on New York's World Trade Center.

As Bolan pushed forward toward the sounds of distant trains, one thing was clear in his mind—any mission that prevented another terrorist attack on the United States was worth his involvement.

The Executioner had been deployed, and he was prepared to give as good as he got.

BOLAN ARRIVED AT THE TRAIN tracks as the first suggestions of predawn light were touching the eastern sky. He estimated he was eight or nine miles away from where he had left his car, but, luckily, the tracks were configured north to south. As long as he jumped a train going the right way, it would bring him closer to his transportation.

He paused at the edge of the woods and, while remaining concealed by the mulberry bushes that populated a narrow gully extending from the trees to the tracks, he reached into the pouch containing his night-vision goggles. With the coming dawn, ambient light was greatly increased and, with it, came maximum visibility.

The SUV that had attacked him at the ambush site was nowhere to be seen and a quick glance around the area explained why. This section of track was as inaccessible to wheeled vehicles as the woods had been. A rushing mountain stream cut through the hilly area to the north and rough outcroppings littered the terrain on the other side of the tracks for as far as Bolan could see.

He heard the sound of a slow freight train coming his way, the steady clack of wheels on the rails indicating a speed that could probably be jumped. Placing the goggles back into their pouch, he headed down the gully to a concealed spot close to the tracks.

The train came around a curve and into sight, going faster than Bolan had originally judged. He remained motionless as the double locomotives reached his position and sailed past at about thirty miles per hour—a little too quick for him to attempt a clean jump.

Remaining hidden under the cover of bushes that grew along the tracks to heights of more than six feet, Bolan opened the pouch on his web belt, which held a grappling hook and a length of special cord developed for its strength. Thin and waxy, the lightweight fiber looked like braided strands of dental floss and, although it had a texture so fine a twenty-foot length could be folded to fit into a shirt pocket, it was stronger than the nylon rope used by mountaineers.

Bolan knotted his titanium grappling hook to the cord, and, while judging the feel of the hook's weight by letting it swing slightly on a few feet of slack, he eyed the passing freight cars for the right opportunity.

More than two dozen boxcars had already passed. A series of double-length flatbeds holding tarp-shrouded cargo came into view. As the cars drew closer, Bolan's eyes searched for possible catching points on the heavy ropes that were lashed across the gray canvas tarps and fastened to metal cleats running along the outside edge of the flatbeds.

Bolan gave the knot a final tug, stepped out from behind the bush and began to run alongside the train. When the first of the flatbeds with the covered freight passed, he increased his speed while whirling the hook over his head like a rodeo cowboy. As he reached a full sprint, he zeroed in on one of the tarp's restraining ropes and let it fly. The grappling hook caught at the very top of the tarp on his first attempt, yanking him up and onward as he tightened his hold on the cord. With the muscles in his shoulders and forearms straining, he jumped and pulled with all his strength, his feet clearing the edge of the moving car with inches to spare. Drawing himself forward on the line, he quickly reeled in the slack and freed the hook, putting it back into its pouch on his web belt.

The tracks were level and in good shape, giving the train a smooth, steady ride. Holding on to the slick surface of the canvas tarp, Bolan moved to the front of the flatbed where there was space for him to sit and rest. He reached a clear spot and settled onto the pitted deck with his back resting against the covered cargo as dawn painted the Irish countryside in crisp morning light.

The terrain was changing, morphing from the barren hostility of the moors to pastures that stretched green and fertile under the rising sun. A rust-flaked trestle came into view up ahead, its blistered surface glowing fiery red in the early light. The structure was a remnant from previous years when trains on this run were used for more than simply transporting freight, but its presence made Bolan consider the safety of his position. As he passed under the trestle's crossbeam, he reasoned that with pastures there would be crossroads, and with the crossroads there would be bridges above the tracks. Unlike the rusting trestle he had just passed under, a bridge could hold an SUV.

Bolan thought his pursuers not only would have known where his escape route from the ambush site would take him, they also would have considered what his options would be once he reached the tracks. As he checked to make sure that both his Desert Eagle and the Beretta were ready for action, he wondered if hopping the train was too obvious.

He calculated he had about fifteen minutes until the tracks began ascending into the mountains along the coast. At that point, he'd get off and walk the rest of the way to his car.

THE SUV'S HIGH PROFILE made it visible from afar. It was sitting on a narrow bridge spanning the tracks, illuminated by the angled rays of the morning sun as if it was on stage. The four men armed with Uzi machine pistols standing in pairs on each side of the vehicle were facing into the sun, putting them at a distinct disadvantage.

Bolan inched to the forward edge of the flatbed and looked around the corner of the cargo loaded onto the car in front of him. Next to the tracks below the SUV, men stood on each side of the passing train, both armed with AK-47s. At the current speed, Bolan estimated he'd be next to them in about three minutes and he'd be exposed for a clean shot from above as well as from both sides.

His eyes darted around the flatbed for a place for him to hide. Even if he got under the tarp, he didn't know if there would be something he could get behind to afford cover from gunfire, but he certainly couldn't stay where he was.

Pulling his combat knife from its sheath, he sliced the closest restraining rope. The freed corner of the tarp flapped up, exposing the bottom half of wooden crates stacked so tightly and neatly against one another there wasn't room for a mouse to crawl between.

As he put the knife away, the Executioner leaned back and looked down, viewing the heavy coupling mechanism linking his car with the one in front. There was a wide space between the clamp and the beginning of his flatbed. With less than a minute and a half remaining before he'd pass under the bridge, Bolan decided the coupler was his only chance for getting past the SUV.

He lowered himself onto the rod between cars, held on tightly to the greasy coupler and slid himself under the flatbed. At first, he thought he'd have to hold his legs up to keep his heels from dragging on the tracks, but once he got under the cargo deck, he discovered there was a beam running across the car about a foot below the flatbed's underside. Bolan slid his legs into the space and found he could balance himself faceup, mere inches below the flatbed's deck. And, although he felt pinned in this position, the supporting beam allowed him free use of both hands.

As the train neared the bridge, he wiped his greasy hands on the front of his shirt before drawing his Beretta from its shoulder leather. With his other hand, he pulled the Desert Eagle from his hip holster.

The flapping tarp caught the attention of the men on both sides of the track. Thinking that Bolan was hiding under the canvas, they began spraying the cargo with gunfire, the cracking of 7.62 mm rounds masked by the sound of the train. With their eyes focused on their target, they stitched holes across the tarp in a crisscrossing pattern from corner to corner, never seeing the man suspended in the dark shadows beneath the railroad car.

As he passed between them, Bolan fired with both hands, his weapons spitting death. The rifleman on the right side was hit inches above his belt with three of the Beretta's 9 mm parabellum rounds. They shoved him backward, his rifle sending a spray of bullets wildly into the air as his finger froze in a death grip on the AK-47's trigger until the magazine was spent and the bolt clicked onto an open chamber. As he stumbled under weak knees into a sitting position, he dropped his weapon, never knowing the origin of the rounds that were ending his life. With a short low scream that turned quickly into a hard grunt, the gunner fell onto his back while clutching his guts in a futile attempt to stem the flow of blood that surged warm and steaming into his hands.

The man on the left was dispatched by two heavy rounds that roared within a millisecond of each other from the mouth of Bolan's Desert Eagle. The steel-jacketed rounds caught the guy midchest, tossing him like a rag doll into the brush alongside the tracks where he landed on his back, arms outstretched.

On the bridge above, the men standing next to the SUV searched for the source of gunfire but, before they could locate it, Bolan's flatbed passed under their position and he became shielded from their weapons by the cargo strapped to the car behind him. Cursing, they scrambled to the other side of the bridge and watched the cars passing underneath. Two of the four opened fire with their Uzis, hosing the flatbeds with a steady stream of 9 mm rounds that sparked and whined as they ricocheted off the metal couplings and tracks.

Once he was beyond their position, Bolan quickly holstered his weapons and pulled himself out from under the railroad car. He peered around the edge of the bullet-riddled canvas in time to see four men dropping from the bridge onto the cargo-laden flatbed three down the line from his. The fixed wooden stocks on their Uzis told Bolan they were carrying older models, but even the earliest versions were formidable killing machines.

The men were obviously planning to work their way forward until they came to Bolan's position. As he visualized his attackers working as a team, covering one another with a forward wall of lead while advancing up both sides of the cargo on each flatbed, Bolan knew there was a strong possibility they'd successfully reach him.

He scrambled to the other side of his car and peered around the corner. A hail of bullets ripped the canvas directly in front of his face, causing him to pull back out of their line of fire. But in the short seconds before he ducked behind cover, he had seen enough to know his pursuers were employing the exact tactic he suspected. One of them had already begun inching along the outside of their cargo load.

A trestle passed overhead, and Bolan began counting. Switching the fire selector on his Beretta to the 3-round burst mode, he reached around the side of the shredded tarp and pressed the trigger, exposing no more than his hand for a few seconds. The triburst forced the gunners to duck, giving him the seconds he needed to sneak another quick look. The man halfway up the side of the flatbed directly behind Bolan's had been hit in the upper chest and was holding on for dear life to a rope laced across the cargo. Bolan fired another 3-round burst, and the man's head exploded in a crimson bloom of brain matter and bone splinters that splashed onto the canvas tarp. As the man's lifeless body slid to the ground, his legs fell at an angle onto the tracks where they were severed by the train's heavy steel wheels as cleanly as if by a guillotine.

A return volley made Bolan pull back behind the cargo, but not before he saw the trestle pass over the end of their car. He had counted to thirty-two from the time the trestle passed over his head until he saw it clear the car where his attackers crouched. He lunged to the other side of his car and fired a few bursts down the left side of the train, reloaded, then jumped back to the right side and repeated the action. For the time being, his opponents were remaining behind the cover of their cargo.

Bolan leaped to his full standing position, grabbing a quick look across the top of the tarps. As he had expected, his movement was met with a blizzard of lead that forced him back down, but not before registering the angle at which one of the men was climbing onto the top of the cargo. With the same technique he had used for the assailant trying to rush the side of the flatbed, Bolan fired above the tarps without looking, thereby giving his foes the smallest target possible by only exposing his hand for the few seconds it took to press the Beretta's trigger. The howls and shrieks of fury immediately reaching his ears told him he had found his mark. Stealing a quick glance over the tarp, he saw his opponent fall from the top of the cargo before the remaining two forced Bolan down with a spray of bullets.

Bolan fingered the remaining magazines in his combat belt while considering his options. By randomly firing quick bursts along the sides and over the top of the cargo loads without giving his enemies more than a second to return fire, Bolan knew he could keep them pinned down, preventing them from rushing his position. It was a classic Mexican standoff, but they had all the time in the world to wait until he ran out of ammo.

Holstering the Beretta, he unhooked an M-68 fragmentation grenade from his web belt and reached into the pouch containing the grappling hook he had used to jump the train. The thin cord was still knotted in place, cinched tight onto the hook by the strain of pulling him on board. While keeping a lookout for the next trestle that the train would pass under, Bolan tied the apple-shaped grenade to the cord's free end, sliding the knot so the hook hung about three feet from the explosive. He set the fuse for slightly longer than thirty seconds, pulled the pin and held the grenade in his right hand while he drew the Beretta with his left.

Scrambling from side to side, he fired 3-round volleys first from the right side, then from the left, keeping his attackers crouched behind the canvas-covered freight loaded onto their flatbed. When the next trestle was passing over him, Bolan tossed the grappling hook above the rusted crossbeam. The grenade's safety lever fell free as the hook looped around the trestle, leaving the M-68 dangling on the thin cord like a tiny piñata a few inches above the flatbed's cargo.

Bolan continued firing on each side of the railroad car to keep his opponents in place while he counted the seconds. When he reached twenty-eight, he looked above the top edge of his tarp and saw that his timing was perfect. The dangling grenade exploded at the exact moment it fell between cars, its thunderous percussion blowing his two enemies from the train.

As the bridge holding the SUV faded into the distance, the Executioner leaned against the boxes of freight and reloaded his Beretta before holstering the weapon. The tracks were beginning to ascend, which meant they were approaching the mountains where he had left his car.

The twin locomotives slowed considerably to cope with the rising grade, giving Bolan ample opportunity to pick an ideal spot to disembark. He hit the ground running, his momentum quickly propelling him away from the train toward a heavily wooded ridge that rose steeply on both sides of the tracks. Having studied topographical maps of the surrounding area before coming in, he knew exactly where he was. Beyond the ridge he now faced, a treacherous coastal road wound up and over the mountains, eventually leading inland to Derry. His car was about a mile up that road.

Bolan leaned into the hillside, rapidly putting distance between himself and the train. As he ran through the woods, he pondered the threat posed by the men in the SUV. He had killed nine of their number, but, judging from their inferiority when engaged in combat, he doubted if they were actual members of the new splinter group threatening the United

States. These men were most likely local hoodlums, hired by the Apprentices for the sole purpose of killing whomever came for Oxford's remains.

Whether or not the survivors would try to find him to avenge their losses was an open question. If they feared they might be killed for failing, or, if payment was contingent on success, they could very well be scouring the roads at this moment, looking for their quarry.

When he came to the edge of the woods where the road began, Bolan dropped to one knee to get his bearings. Rather than proceed on the asphalt where he could be surprised by a vehicle coming around one of numerous blind corners, he decided he would remain about ten yards into the woods. Out of habit, he did a quick touch-check of his weapons before heading off.

It took about fifteen minutes to reach the spot where his Land Rover sat, pulled safely off the road in one of the deep cutouts into the cliff. The vehicle was as Bolan had left it the evening before, a red dashboard light blinking a pattern that told him the car had remained untouched.

As he put the car into gear and pulled out of the cutout onto the road, he glanced at his watch. 6:00 a.m., and the sun was high in the sky.

The tires of the Land Rover gripped the weathered blacktop, propelling him upward on the twisty mountain road. Even with the surface dry and clean, going was dangerous. The asphalt hugged the side of the mountain like a ribbon pulled taut, with turns so tight that no more than a hundred feet of road was visible at any given time. To make matters worse, the grade was getting steeper, affording heart-stopping views over the side of the mountain where hundreds of feet below, surf crashed in a bluish green foam against the rocks.

It was during one of the jackknife turns that hung out over

the water, giving Bolan a view of the road winding along the mountainside below him, that he saw the SUV. It was about a quarter of the way down the mountain, coming fast on a straight stretch before it turned out of sight to twist and meander before it would emerge on the road a little higher.

Not knowing if they had spotted him, Bolan increased his pressure on the gas pedal. The vehicle surged forward, spitting loose gravel off to the side. He was about five miles from the spot where the road turned inland. Once he got there, he'd be able to open up and leave his pursuers in the dust.

He rounded a curve, his back tires sliding into a fishtail. Bolan tapped lightly on the brakes to control the skid as a 90 mm rocket whizzed by ten feet in front of him. The projectile slammed into the hillside, sending an explosion of small boulders and dirt into the road. Bolan swerved to avoid the rockfall, his tires screaming as they lay heavy rubber tracks onto the tar while grabbing for traction.

The SUV was on a flat vista higher up the mountain than Bolan thought it would be, making him realize his enemies were in a faster vehicle than his. His original plan to speed away once the trail became level needed serious revision. Finding himself out on a flat track in front of a faster vehicle armed with rockets was not a scenario Bolan could allow to develop.

The road twisted out over the water, and Bolan touched the gas pedal to race around the exposed curve. As he did, he glanced to the cutout vista on the mountainside below. A man knelt next to the SUV, a 90 mm recoilless rifle resting on his shoulder. He fired, and a fireball flashed from the end of the tube. The sound reached Bolan's ears a second later, only to be immediately swallowed by the eardrum-throbbing explosion occurring three feet behind his vehicle as his quick burst of speed whipped the Land Rover around the corner and out of sight.

With a faster vehicle and heavy armament, Bolan's enemies held the upper hand. His mind racing, he hugged the edge of the mountain as he sped into a straightaway leading to another curve extending out over the water.

Bolan came through the curve, immediately after which the road turned sharply upward next to a large grotto. It was almost as deep as the one where he'd left the Land Rover the night before, and, as soon as he passed, Bolan stomped on the brakes. The vehicle skidded and shimmied to a spot just past the cutout. Bolan dumped the transmission into Reverse and pealed backward into the grotto, the hood of his vehicle extending a few feet onto the blacktop. If he went straight forward, he'd cross the road and go over the cliff.

Bolan put the car into Park, got out and slammed his shoulder into the side mirror, snapping it off. Using his combat knife, he cut the wires protruding from the mirror assembly and pulled it free.

The sound of the ocean crashing into the rocky shore hundreds of feet below could be heard when he ran into the middle of the road where he positioned the mirror. He sprinted back behind the curve and crouched next to the Land Rover and looked into the mirror's reflection. It was placed correctly to give him a view around the corner of the road approaching the bend.

Bolan opened the driver's door and, while kneeling next to the car and leaning in, wedged his combat knife between the accelerator and seat so that the gas pedal was pushed to the floor. As the engine raced, he pressed down on the brake with all his strength and shifted into Drive, holding the car's horsepower in check with one arm. Keeping his eyes riveted to the reflection in the mirror he had placed in the middle of the road, he held steady while beads of sweat broke out across his brow.

The kill would be quick, one way or the other. The SUV would come tearing around the corner. If Bolan was fast enough, he'd release the Land Rover's brake, allowing his vehicle to bolt from the cutout and crash into his pursuers as they came abreast, knocking them over the side. It was a desperate plan that required perfect timing.

The Land Rover lurched forward an inch, and Bolan pressed harder on the brake pedal, his muscles cramping under the strain. Drops of stinging sweat trickled into his eyes as he waited patiently for his enemies. Despite the agony that screamed from within his arm and shoulder, he willed himself to push harder, controlling the car that surged under his hands like an energy-charged Thoroughbred at the starting gate.

The SUV suddenly appeared in the mirror, coming fast around the curve. A split second later, it was in front of the grotto, its engine racing against the elevation. Bolan released the brake and fell backward as his vehicle surged forward, smashing into the SUV's passenger side.

Shrieks of twisting metal and screaming tires filled the air. The Land Rover roared forward, pushing the SUV sideways. The vehicle's driver reacted to the surprise crash by hitting his brakes, which had the effect of giving the Land Rover better leverage as it thrust forward, back tires spinning and smoking, propelling the vehicle toward the edge of the cliff.

When the entwined cars reached the brink, they balanced precariously above the void, as if deciding whether to go over the side. In the SUV's backseat, two men, their faces reflecting the terror of their situation, began scrambling over each other in an attempt to find the door handle on the side not smashed by the Land Rover. But, before they could grasp it, the laws of physics intervened and the two vehicles plunged over the side, falling through the air for three or four long seconds before crashing onto the rocks below. There was a brief silence before both cars exploded, generating sound waves that merged and echoed as one across the Irish countryside.

Bolan rose from his position and peered over the edge. He was sweaty and breathing hard, but he had bested the enemy. Sliding his hand into his shirt pocket, he fingered Oxford's molar and the three medals he had taken from the men at the ambush site.

He had won this particular battle, but the Executioner had no doubt that this war was just beginning.

Stony Man Farm, Virginia

Less than twenty-four hours after returning from Ireland, Mack Bolan sat with Hal Brognola at a conference table in the War Room, one level below Stony Man Farm. Also with them were Carmen Delahunt and Akira Tokaido—two-thirds of Aaron, the Bear, Kurtzman's cybernetics team.

While waiting for the rest of the group to arrive, Bolan scanned his copy of the message Agent Steven Oxford had Morse-coded minutes before his death into the microchip implanted in his molar.

"Hot off the press," Delahunt said, nodding toward the transcript. "Good job, Tokaido, decoding it before they even gave us the key."

Tokaido shrugged while snapping his ever-present bubble gum. "No challenge," he said while tonguing the pink wad into the space between his teeth and right cheek. He stared into space, head nodding slightly to the rock music blasting through his earbuds, and added, "CIA," in a derisive tone that conveyed his disdain for what he considered inferior programming and encryption.

"This was their first mention of going after the CIA?" Bolan asked, without looking up from his reading.

"According to Oxford it was," Brognola answered. "But let's wait until the others get here."

As if on cue, the doors to the elevator built into the corner of the room slid open on a silent cushion of air and an attractive woman, who Bolan judged to be in her early thirties, stepped out. She was about five foot nine with jet black hair that fell straight to her shoulders, framing an ivory-pure angelic face. An off-white silk blouse tucked into pleated black slacks hugged her slender curves in an attractive but not provocative way. The woman's sparkling blue eyes swept quickly across the War Room, settling for a moment on Bolan before moving on to the others.

Aaron Kurtzman was right behind her, holding the door back with one hand for the woman to exit the elevator ahead of him while he gripped a cup of his lethally strong coffee with the other, ever the gentleman, despite being confined to a wheelchair.

Last off the elevator was Huntington Wethers, the distinguished-looking ex-UCLA professor whose academic approach to research was a perfect complement to Tokaido's natural hacker skills and Delahunt's methodical commonsense methods.

"Katey," Brognola said, rising from his chair as the woman approached.

"That's quite the confidentiality contract you've got, Hal. Twenty-five years in Leavenworth for even a minor violation? And the President endorsed it." The woman shook her head in disbelief.

"It's in the best interest of national security. Now, have you met everyone?" Brognola asked.

Her eyes fell again on Bolan, who stood and extended his hand.

"Matt Cooper," he said, using the cover name he'd recently acquired.

"Katey Adams."

Her grip was firm, and the way she moved made Bolan suspect she probably had an athletic background.

She had, in fact, been one of the most ferocious field-hockey forwards ever to graduate from MIT, but her most significant athletic achievement during her four years at the institute—and the one that initially caught the interest of the CIA recruiters—was her performance on the school's pistol team for which she earned All-Ivy honors her senior year.

"Katey is on loan to us from the White House Protocol Section," Brognola said while everyone got settled. "Until last year, when Edmund Fontes took over, she was head of the CIA's Irish operation, a post she held for eight years. As such, she's their foremost expert on Ireland. Katey?"

She began by asking, "Have you all had time to read Agent Oxford's transcript?"

There were nods around the table.

"Have Randolph's agents been warned?" Bolan asked.

"Too late for that," she answered. "Marie Johnston was killed this morning in Pamplona at about two o'clock our time. We just didn't get the molar soon enough. Taylor and Buckley were both hit yesterday. Randolph has been warned. He's back at his home base in Stuttgart after taking a few days of leave."

Wethers emitted a low whistle. "Where were the other two killed?" he asked.

"Taylor in London, Buckley in Paris," Adams replied.

"Is it possible the killings aren't connected?" Tokaido asked. "A coincidence of three, even with the communiqué, doesn't equate to zero probability."

Bolan thought he could hear a tinny sound coming from the hacker's earbuds and wondered how the man could follow a conversation above the racket.

"Ballistics confirmed that the same weapon killed all three," Adams answered. "There was also an orange scarf left with each body."

"They want us to know it's them," Brognola said. "Clearly, the group who sent Fontes the communiqué is the same one killing Randolph's agents."

"But are they really backed by the Orange Order?" Delahunt asked. Looking over the frame of her tortoiseshell glasses at Kurtzman, who sat directly across the table from her, she added, "Anyone can plant a few scarves."

"The Orange Order denies involvement," Adams said in support of Delahunt's thought.

"But it would be good for them if the demands in the communiqué were met," Kurtzman said.

"Of course it would. IRA disarmament and irrefutable establishment of Northern Ireland? It would end the conflict. But there's no way it'll happen like this. If terrorists attack the United States, we won't negotiate with them. We'll retaliate like we did against the Taliban in Afghanistan." Adams paused for a moment, as if for emphasis, before saying, "As soon as we can reasonably link someone to these agent killings, we're sending Fontes a strike force to wipe out their network."

There was silence around the table for a few moments while the team considered the actual evidence they had. It wasn't much.

Kurtzman took a sip of coffee, gazing from face to face above the rim of his cup as he did so. "There are two questions, in particular, we must answer. First, why kill Marie Johnston? Taylor and Buckley were field agents, but Johnston was nothing more than an interpreter."

"Because it's not about the mission," Delahunt replied, her words eliciting nods of agreement.

"Secondly," Kurtzman continued in his patient, thoughtful manner, "is it plausible that a terrorist cell in Northern Ireland would have the means to attack the United States? We're not talking a global organization like al Qaeda here. What's the worst thing a breakaway group of the Orange Order could do?"

"Dirty bomb," Tokaido said.

Delahunt leaned forward, said, "Anthrax mailings," and then added in a rush, "You bet your ass they have the means. Maybe not for something as dramatic as 9/11, but a subway explosion, a dirty bomb, biological attacks—you don't need a global infrastructure to pull off any of those."

"But there are always clues ahead of time if you know where to look," Tokaido said.

Kurtzman smiled, the pride he felt for his team evident on his face.

"What do you think about these?" Brognola asked no one in particular while reaching into his shirt pocket and tossing onto the table the three chains Bolan had pulled from his would-be ambushers the previous night. "Scapular medals. They lead me to believe that the three men guarding Oxford's body were Catholics. The Orange Order is a Protestant group."

"They were thugs," Bolan answered. "Local hired help. Most likely not part of the core organization. We can't draw any conclusions from those medals. Not without more intel."

Wethers suddenly said, "They're going to hit Randolph tomorrow."

Before his colleagues could ask him to elaborate, he eplained, "Taylor in London, Buckley in Paris, Johnston in Pamplona. Look at a map and the time between killings. Randolph in Stuttgart is the next element in an obviously clear progression. One killer is making a circular sweep. Plus, we have Oxford's transcript that says it was all coming down this week."

"Katey is going back to Ireland," Brognola said, "and, while she's there, Cooper will go to Stuttgart to debrief Randolph. If Hunt is right," he added, looking straight at Bolan, "it will be good for you to be there regardless of anything Randolph can tell you about his previous missions. He's used Ireland as a gateway for defectors three times. Maybe he stepped on some toes during one of them."

"You're not suggesting someone other than Cypher is behind these hits," Bolan said, more a statement than a question. "I agree with Hunt. Oxford's message is clear. Cypher is the enemy. The question is, who is he? Oxford was undercover for more than a year, but Cypher doesn't show up in his reports until three months ago. Where did this guy come from?"

Brognola had been involved with Bolan long enough to know that the man's question was not rhetorical. The Executioner was on the hunt and there would be no rest until he found his answer. More likely than not, along the way, there would be hell to pay.

TEN HOURS AFTER HER MEETING with the team at Stony Man Farm, Katey Adams looked away from the window of the Hawker Horizon as it shot across the night sky. There was nothing outside for her to see. Ireland's southwest shoreline was still almost an hour away. When they landed, it would be four in the morning, local time.

Adams sighed and turned toward the man napping in the oversized leather seat across the tiny aisle from her.

The first thing she had noticed about him when she'd stepped off the elevator at Stony Man Farm was how broad his shoulders were. And he was tall, easily six-three or -four. But the trait that had kept her looking back—and, if truth be told, she had fought the urge to stare throughout the entire meeting—was the intelligence that burned in his eyes so intensely that she wondered if they could peer straight into her soul.

He stirred and turned toward her in his sleep. His hair was cut short, but there was a lock in front that had slipped out of place, and Adams wanted very much to reach over and push it back.

His eyes snapped open, making her jump.

"We're almost there. About an hour," she said, recovering from having been caught staring. "I've always hated this flight."

He pushed himself upright in the chair and rubbed his face with his hands.

"It's not a problem for you to leave your job?" he asked as if there had been no break in the hour-long conversation they had shared upon takeoff.

"Actually, it is. The President wants his cabinet to hit the campaign trail, and I'm in charge of planning some of the trips. Daniel Foley's visiting West Point next month. That'll be a biggie, and I do have to get back to finish the advance work. I can't stay in Ireland for more than a few days."

"There's no one you can give your work to?"

Adams shrugged. "I guess I could, but ever since 9/11, we've kept the specifics of cabinet trips secret until the very last moment. I'm the only one who knows the details of Foley's and a few other itineraries, and passing them off at this point and trying to bring someone else up to speed might actually be harder than just getting them done myself. Especially in light of these new threats."

"Tell me about the guy you're going to visit."

Adams smiled as she thought of Bryan McGuinness, the fiery editor of the *Irish Independent,* who had all but adopted her during her first year as CIA section chief in Dublin.

"We go way back, me and Bryan. When I was new in Ireland, he went out of his way to show me the good places to eat, to introduce me to the right people and just to make me feel at home. He did a lot of favors for me in those eight years."

"Never asked anything in return?"

Adams shook her head. "I know what you're thinking. I had him checked out when he kept pushing himself on me, and he is a member of the IRA, but we already knew that from his editorials. He never asked me to compromise myself in any way."

The copilot spread the curtain separating the cockpit from the cabin and, without getting up from his seat, announced, "We're starting our descent. After landing, we'll take a two-hour break to refuel and get something to eat before going on to Stuttgart."

"Okay," Adams answered as the man turned back to the controls and said something into his headset mike that made the pilot next to him nod and grin.

"Good luck in Ireland," Bolan said while fastening his seat belt.

Adams responded in kind, and then they were silent, each lost in his or her own thoughts about the upcoming assignments, until the plane touched down at Shannon airport.

Stuttgart, Germany

The sun was low in the east, throwing the life-sized chessmen into stark relief against a bright green background of closely cropped lawns. Long, straight shadows cast by the chess pieces stretched across the marble chessboard, some reaching beyond the board's sandstone border to touch manicured edges of grass. From behind the secluded bench on which Mack Bolan sat, Asian day lilies in well-tended beds filled the early-morning air with a cloying fragrance.

Bolan's position gave him a good view of the rolling lawns with their flower-lined walkways meandering like serpentine tributaries through randomly spaced clumps of trees toward a stand of thick pines about a quarter of a mile away. Except for a small flock of sparrows pecking the ground under a few benches and three maintenance men off to his left, cultivating a clump of short azaleas, the park was deserted.

Brognola had told Bolan that Peter Randolph's daily routine included a walk to work through the commons and, despite the field agent's flat refusal of his offer to provide protection, Bolan was sitting out of sight behind a clump of birches about thirty yards from the huge chessboard, watching for Randolph's approach.

He unzipped his lightweight golf jacket so he could touch-check the fire-selector switch on his Beretta 93-R. Brognola had arranged for it to pass through customs. Unlike France and all of Scandinavia, Germany was one of the easier European countries to enter with weapons. Counting the 20-round magazine, already locked into the high-performance pistol, and the four spare clips he carried in his jacket pockets, Bolan was packing one hundred rounds of 9 mm parabellum ammunition.

A fat bumblebee hovered close, its heavy drone filling the air like electricity under high-tension wires. As Bolan waved the insect away, he noticed movement between two clumps of waist-high zinnias about a hundred yards down one of the walkways. Even from that distance, he could tell it was Randolph, hands in his pockets, strolling casually through the multicolored flowers.

Realizing that the three gardeners he had noticed minutes earlier were nowhere in sight, Bolan eased himself off the bench while drawing his Beretta from its shoulder holster. Eyes sweeping the park, he stepped forward into the cover offered by the small grove of birches.

The scent of freshly mowed grass filled his nostrils and the air seemed almost crisp enough to touch. The memory of sitting next to a photographer in a Maui bar flashed through Bolan's mind. The man had told him that early-morning and late-afternoon light, when the rays were coming in soft and low to the horizon, was the best for shooting intense, saturated colors. With his senses on full alert, registering the flower beds, the lawns and Randolph drawing closer to the chessmen, Bolan understood what the photographer had meant.

The flock of sparrows took to flight with a ruffling sound a split second before the air was filled with the abrupt stutter of automatic fire. The birds gave Randolph—whose carefree demeanor had obviously been a ruse—the alarm he needed, and he threw himself to the ground without a moment's hesitation as the first flurry of rounds zipped above him. Two of the gardeners had taken cover behind outcroppings and the third had settled himself among a group of small moguls that dotted a section of lawn like baby mountains. Their positions created a lazy triangle allowing them to pin Randolph with intersecting fire.

Bolan rushed to the edge of the birches, firing his Beretta in 3-round bursts. His presence caught the gunmen by surprise and, before his first magazine was half spent, he drilled a hole through the jaw of the closest gardener who was on one knee hosing the area around Randolph with 9 mm rounds blazing from the business end of a Heckler & Koch MP-5 machine pistol. The man opened his lips as if to scream, but any final sound he intended to make was blocked by the scarlet geyser erupting through his mouth and nose. He toppled sideways to the ground, where his body convulsed for a few seconds with bone-rattling shudders before coming to rest.

The two remaining gunmen redirected their fire at Bolan, shredding the brittle birch branches above him into thousands of pieces that rained onto his back and shoulders like black confetti. He dived into a bed of mulch behind a tight trio of trees, inhaling a nostril full of redwood dust that puffed up around his face in a dirty cloud when he landed.

While the gunmen were busy throwing a reciprocating wall of lead at Bolan, Randolph took the opportunity to scramble on all fours to a safer spot behind a small mound of bloodred calla lilies in full bloom. He quickly entered the fray with a series of single shots from his Smith & Wesson .357 Magnum. His action was met with a responsive barrage of fire that sent him ducking for cover behind the mound.

Bolan ejected his spent magazine and rammed a fresh

one home. Realizing that the thin trees affording him cover could not withstand a prolonged assault of automatic fire, he searched for a better position. The chessmen were approximately six seconds away—an eternity when rounds were snapping the air all around you—but he couldn't stay where he was. He pushed himself to his feet and rushed toward the life-sized pieces, firing his Beretta as he ran. When he reached a point about ten yards from the row of pawns, he launched himself into a horizontal dive, squeezing the trigger of his Beretta as rapidly as he could. A round creased his back just below his shoulder blades and he felt the hot sting of a flesh wound milliseconds before he landed hard on the chessboard. The space immediately surrounding him was filled with the sickening whine of ricochets as fist-sized chunks of granite exploded from the black king's chest, clattering onto the marble squares next to where he lay.

When Bolan chanced a look around the edge of the tombstone-high pawn giving him the cover he needed, he discovered that the man positioned among the moguls was out of his line of fire, obscured from sight by the gentle mounds of grass-covered earth that Bolan's new spot placed between them. Lowering the Beretta's front grip and loading a full magazine, he prepared to take on the gunman he could see, hoping to eliminate him before his partner came to his aid.

As if in concert with Bolan's thoughts, Randolph began laying down covering fire. Bolan rose to one knee behind the chess piece, firing. Sizzling hot brass poured from the smoking ejector port in a parabolic arc that shone gold in the early-morning light.

The gunman under fire made an ill-timed decision to dash for a better spot, and the Executioner caught him first in the thigh, then stitched him from waist to neck with six fatal rounds.

A round screamed past Bolan's head less than an arm's

length away, the tone of the snap as the bullet sped by telling him it had come from behind. He threw himself prone, searching for the new gunman. There was open space all the way to the clump of pines.

The park suddenly became deathly silent. In the distance, the sound of police sirens signaled the imminent arrival of German law-enforcement personnel.

"Randolph!" Bolan shouted.

"Yeah."

"Can you see them?"

"I think they're gone."

Randolph sprinted from his position behind the lilies to the chessboard, where he dived behind the black pawns, then crawled his way to Bolan's spot. The dash behind the pawn had drawn no gunfire from either direction.

Randolph remained focused to the front, Bolan to the rear. A full thirty seconds passed, with the sirens drawing closer.

"I think they're gone," Randolph repeated.

Bolan nodded.

"You're hit."

"Just a scrape."

"Cover me."

Randolph ran in a half crouch to one of the dead men, turned and shouted, "We got all three."

Some combat veterans developed a sense for knowing when a firefight was over. Bolan was one of them. He stood and took a few steps forward, confident that whomever had been concealed in the pines was gone. As he approached Randolph, he stretched and flexed his shoulders in an attempt to assess the damage to his back. It was barely noticeable.

The gunman who had taken cover among the moguls was lying faceup, arms stretched to the side as if he had been crucified. A substantial head wound was the obvious cause of death. Tucked in his belt was a .22-caliber Ruger pistol, and Bolan could see an orange scarf poking out of his pants pocket.

"I thought this one ran," Randolph said, motioning to the corpse while walking up to Bolan. "I must have hit him with a ricochet."

He got down on his knees and began checking the dead man's pockets. "You should get out of here before the police arrive. I have a relationship with them. We'll get our guys to clean up."

"Make sure ballistics matches all the killer rounds."

"Will do. Hey—" he looked up from going through the dead man's pockets "—thanks, by the way."

The sirens were very close. Bolan took a long last look at the clump of pines in the distance before turning and walking away.

Rain pelted down, rendering the city a chilly gray. Bryan McGuinness looked out from his third-story window in the northeast corner of the *Irish Independent* offices to the wet street below. Neon store signs reflecting in psychedelic colors off the slick pavement danced a squiggly step as elusive as peace. Through the downpour, McGuinness could barely make out the flashing lights in front of the Bank of Ireland: 1420…08 JUL…21.1C

Another anniversary. Almost every date, he realized with a heavy sigh, had become one. Birthdays and death days. They filled his calendar.

He coughed, a loose rattling sound, and reached into his shirt pocket for a cigarette.

The eighth was one of Kevin's dates. Ten months to the day, another life wasted.

McGuinness lit the cigarette and took a deep drag while forcing himself to think about his brother. Memories were all he had now. It was important he keep them alive.

Ten months, and his brother's death had accomplished nothing. The British were still in Ireland; Kevin would never see his twenty-first birthday, never be allowed to grow into the man God had given him the talents to become. The soldiers had made sure of that when they'd gunned him down like a mad dog in the street. They'd said he was running from the Palace Barracks where he and his friends had been planting explosives—a claim McGuinness doubted.

He knew Kevin had been a member of the IRA. But the editor's sources had told him that his brother was nothing more than a gunrunner, supplying arms to the Falls Road neighborhood in Belfast. He shouldn't have come into direct contact with the enemy.

He watched the rain running like tears down the outside of his window while his mind wandered a million miles away, recalling the talks he and Kevin had shared over pints at the Old Sheiling. His younger brother had made him proud, coming home for the summer from Trinity, his head filled with ideas for tomorrow's Ireland. He had even quoted Bryan's eitorials when arguing unity with the Sheiling's patrons. McGuinness knew the lad deserved better than what he got.

Shaking himself from his reverie, McGuinness glanced down the street at the clock. It was almost time for his visitor.

There was a soft knock on the door.

"Yes?" he asked, turning from the window.

The office door cracked open barely enough for his secretary to stick her head in and say, "Bryan, dear, there's a Katherine Adams here to see you."

"Aye, Margaret, I've been expecting her."

His secretary left to fetch the visitor, and the editor pushed his sorrow to the back of his mind while shifting his extroverted personality into high gear.

When Katherine Adams walked into his office, he was struck, as he always had been, by her flawless beauty. That raven hair above those crystal-clear blue eyes, her perfectly pure skin, the confident manner with which she carried herself—she was a classic Irish beauty, and her very presence made the newsman's heart skip a beat.

"Katherine! Katherine, my dear!" His voice filled the office as he approached her, arms extended. "God bless, 'tis good seeing you."

"Hello, Bryan. Thank you for meeting me on such short notice."

They hugged as old friends and, once they had broken their embrace, McGuinness steered her toward the sofa next to his desk.

"You weren't particular when you rang us up," he said while making his way to a small cabinet next to the window. "Are you back for a time?"

Before she could answer, he opened the bottom door of the cabinet and withdrew a bottle of Jameson's whiskey and two short Waterford drinking glasses.

"Have a spot?"

Adams grinned, said, "Still the same old Bryan."

She accepted three fingers of the dark amber liquid, which shimmered and sparkled behind the crystal, and settled herself onto the sofa's worn leather cushions.

McGuinness walked around his desk and, once he was seated, raised his glass.

"You're here on business?" he asked, a note of sadness in his voice.

"I am. I can't stay long. And I don't know if you're exactly the right person to see, but I think you may have the, ah—" she paused for a moment "—the contacts who might be able to help me."

McGuinness almost choked midswallow. "You haven't lost your way with the blarney," he replied through a smile. "You need a contact now, do you? How can I help?"

Adams took a sip of her whiskey, enjoying the oak aftertaste despite the way it caused her to grimace, and said, "Three CIA agents who finished working on a defection in

Ireland a few weeks ago have been killed. Do you still have access to good information?"

McGuinness winked in the midst of lighting a cigarette. He took a deep drag and answered while blowing out the match with his first exhale. "I'll be connected till the day I meet St. Peter."

He shook his mane of thick black hair and peered at Adams from beneath great bushy eyebrows. "Tell me the tale, my friend."

Adams told McGuinness everything she knew about the murdered agents, the communiqué that had been delivered to Fontes and forwarded to the President and the assistance the CIA was receiving from special agents, the details of which she kept to herself.

Throughout the narrative, McGuinness sat quietly behind his desk, expressionless, chain-smoking cigarettes, pausing now and then to take a sip of his drink. Adams had observed him like this on many occasions—appearing disinterested, seemingly preoccupied, when, in reality, he was deeply concentrating, absorbing and processing every detail.

Adams finished speaking and a silence filled the room.

"Violence," McGuinness said softly, "breeds violence. The British came into Ireland to oppress our people. The IRA was a direct reaction to that force."

He held his palms up and, in a contrite voice, said, "I'm not rationalizing the Army's tactics, mind you. But it's the logical reaction to British violence. And our violence here breeds violence in the North. Every day, we hear of new groups splintering off from the Order to add their bloody efforts to the toil. Every day, it becomes a bit more mad."

"And the South then reacts to the new groups with more violence? Where in hell does it all end?" Adams asked.

Their eyes met for a few seconds before he answered.

"In hell, indeed, my dear. We're caught in an escalating spiral while the diplomats in Parliament sit on their fat arses, leaving the militants to find a solution. Soldiers will always escalate death. It's their livelihood."

He looked beyond Adams into the distance.

"I've heard," he said in a suddenly weary voice, "that a new group has devised a plot to force the United States and England to permanently recognize Northern Ireland as an independent nation."

Adams nodded at the confirmation that his people had heard about the communiqué.

"Rumor has it," he said, "that they've also initiated an international campaign directed against prominent Catholics. There's an assassination list circulating up North that includes the Pope, the two Irish-American members of your President's cabinet and a handful of other people, including Bryan McGuinness."

He smiled wanly, adding, "At least, I'm in good company."

"Are you sure?" Adams whispered, her voice infused with concern, not only at the new revelation, but also that her friend was among those being targeted.

"More certain that I'd like to be."

"But Foley has never taken a public stand on Ireland, and Moore isn't even Catholic," Adams said, as if she could disprove the entire threat—and, with it, the danger to McGuinness—through logic. "And how does it tie in with the CIA agents? Why would they be on the same assassination list? None of this makes sense."

McGuinness held up his hand. "Slow down. One question at a time."

He took a sip of whiskey, swishing it slowly through his mouth before swallowing.

"First off, do not assume that your enemy is logical. The

murdered agents may have been killed simply to show that those behind the communiqué are to be taken seriously. If that be the killers' purpose, they've succeeded now, haven't they? You've been dispatched to Ireland, and the President has assigned special agents to help the CIA. And now you know of a unit sponsored by the Order, and you know that they've named two members of your President's cabinet as future targets. Further demands may come next. Or no."

"It can't be," Adams said. "Terrorism won't get them what they want."

McGuinness paused before answering.

"If they succeed with the assassinations," he said slowly, "Protestant terrorists around the world will rally to their cause. Do you remember the celebrations in the Muslim world following 9/11? There are many places outside of Ireland where Catholics battle Protestants.

"But, most importantly, the United States will immediately pressure England to solve the Irish problem, once and for all. And, if they're pushed hard enough, Parliament will authorize certain economic and military powers to crush our Catholic resistance. Total disarmament of the Republican Army. Something the Good Friday Accords were unable to effect. It won't be a popular action, mind you, but Parliament will say the Americans forced them to do it. And, with the IRA disarmed, the loyalists will win home rule."

Adams shook her head. "It doesn't hang. I can't believe anyone up North is planning to assassinate two American cabinet members, one of whom isn't even Catholic."

"You can't believe or don't want to?" he countered. "Moore's family is a few generations removed, but Foley's grandparents on both sides came from County Kerry. The Order fears his family connections. Seeing the way America dispatched the Taliban and Saddam Hussein, they believe it's only a matter of time before Foley convinces your President to turn his forces against terrorism everywhere, including Ireland. And on what side do you think he would come down? The North is afraid your President may convince England to unite Ireland. Better they gamble now by throwing everything into the till."

He picked up the bottle of whiskey and offered it to Adams, who declined with a shake of her head, before pouring himself another glass.

"I hear Gregory is overseeing the plan and he's assembling a strike team somewhere around Londonderry. Our people are chasing leads as we speak."

The CIA woman's jaw set in a hard line at the mere mention of the legendary vigilante who had terrorized the IRA during her last three years in Ireland. She looked into her lap, massaging her temples with the tips of her fingers.

"Don't they know we'll preempt them if we believe they're coming after a cabinet member?" she asked, almost to herself. "We can't afford to sit back and wait for them to strike. Nine-eleven taught us that."

McGuinness studied his pretty friend, took another sip of whiskey and breathed a silent prayer.

"Are you free for dinner tonight?" he asked. "Let me talk a bit to our people and get an update for you. How long are you staying?"

She shook her head absently, preoccupied with the analysis raging through her head. A cabinet assassination? It was insanity. She was in charge of planning campaign trips for the cabinet members barnstorming the Northeast. Foley was one of hers, scheduled to visit West Point in mid-August. Five weeks away.

"Oh," she said, realizing McGuinness was waiting for an answer, "yeah, dinner would be good. But I don't want to stay out late."

"Seven? I'll come to your hotel? We'll go somewhere close by."

She gave him her room number, they hugged goodbye and she left the offices of the *Irish Independent.* It had stopped raining and, with the sun breaking its way through scattering clouds, Adams decided to enjoy the next hour walking through one of her favorite cities.

TREKKING UP BAGGOT STREET on the way to her hotel, Adams had a lively bounce to her step as she passed the upscale shops and eateries. Dublin reminded her in many ways of Boston, with its old churches and brownstones built alongside a river that ran straight through the city. A large population of students in evidence at all hours on the streets was a further similarity to her old college town.

As she had hoped, the stroll was clearing her mind, reducing some of the tensions from her meeting. There was a process to intelligence gathering—discovery, verification and mitigation. Brognola's team would work with her, and they'd get to the bottom of this threat. The only question was if they'd be able to do it in time to prevent an international tragedy.

She passed the statue of Patrick Kavanagh, the slightly larger-than-life bronze figure sitting on a park bench by the bridge where it's said the poet composed most of his work. A group of Asian students were sharing the space next to him, laughing and photographing one another in various poses with the Irish bard. She paused to watch, the sad longing in her soul a reminder that she had once been as carefree as they.

Her metamorphosis into a State Department lifer had happened so gradually she barely noticed when the other parts of her life were slipping away. Her involvement with Robert had ended when they finally admitted their careers were taking them in opposite directions. Her slow but sure estrangement from her mother and sister occurred because they couldn't compete with the excitement of international assignments. She had told herself she'd mend those bridges and get back in touch, but time marched on and the distance fostered distance. At thirty-two years old, Katey Adams was as alone as she was beautiful.

As she approached the Shelbourne, a grand Georgian Hotel located on St. Stephen's Green in one of Dublin's busiest quarters, she forced herself to stop her guilt-driven reminiscing. With McGuinness scheduled to pick her up for dinner in two hours, there was just enough time for her to shower, change clothes and call Brognola for their daily debrief.

Outside the hotel, a street musician was strumming a barely recognizable tune on an old guitar under the rapt gaze of a young woman who appeared to be roughly his age. The woman tenderly touched his neck and shoulders, speaking softly as he pulled clunker after clunker from the instrument. It's often been said that love is blind, but, in this case, Adams thought as she rummaged through her purse for a few euros to toss into the open guitar case in front of the pair, it was also deaf.

"Thank you, m'lady," the singer said, stopping midtune. "Do you have a request?"

Adams smiled and shook her head. "No. Anything is okay."

"You're an American," he said, and, without waiting for a reply, began strumming a few vaguely familiar chords that, once he and his girlfriend began singing, Katey was able to identify as "Misty."

She stayed through the first stanza, but it was hard on the ears and, with a smile and another euro, she waved and hustled herself into the hotel.

THE WATER WAS HOT, and Adams enjoyed the way the needles stung her travel-weary body. She soaped herself all over, working the hotel's lavender-scented soap into a rich lather before rinsing clean. Letting her mind go blank, she stood under the soothing jets for a few minutes, breathing the steam.

Despite her wish to remain in the relaxing warmth, she turned off the tap and reached beyond the shower curtain to the heated wall rack for one of the Shelbourne's extraheavy bath towels. Prior to pushing the curtain aside, she wrapped herself in the thick terry cloth luxury, enjoying its cozy embrace.

The moment she stepped through the doorway into her bedroom, Adams sensed something was wrong. Too late, her senses leaped to full alert a millisecond before the person standing behind the open bathroom door grabbed her around the waist with one arm while forcing a sweet-smelling cloth against her face.

Adams resisted as best she could, but her attacker was very strong. She felt herself going limp in his arms as she tumbled backward into darkness.

“Put something over her,” Cypher said, entering the room and locking the door behind him.

The CIA agent was lying faceup on the bed, arms at her sides, her head and shoulders supported by pillows.

“Why not enjoy the scenery while we work?”

“Cover her up,” he repeated, anger suddenly evident in his tone.

William Palmer retrieved the towel from the floor outside the bathroom and draped it from neck to knees over her naked body. “Satisfied?”

Cypher didn’t respond. He was holding a hypodermic syringe in one hand and a small glass bottle of sodium pentothal in the other. His suppliers had told him the truth serum came from a residual KGB warehouse in Paris and had been quality tested as he’d instructed. While cradling the bottle in his left palm, he used his index finger and thumb to pull the pink plastic sheath from the needle, dropping it onto the bedspread. Raising the bottle to eye level, he inserted the gleaming point through the rubber seal and drew 5 cc into the cartridge.

“Okay,” he said, taking a step forward, “hold her arm.”

Palmer turned the woman’s arm outward to expose the vein. Cypher inserted the needle into the bend at her elbow and pushed the plunger with a slow, steady stroke, squirting the chemicals directly into her bloodstream.

"How long do we wait?" Palmer asked as Cypher withdrew the needle.

"There's a sedative mixed in with the serum, so she'll be out for a few hours, but we should be ready to start in about ten minutes."

Neither man was accustomed to waiting. Cypher smoked and paced the length of the room while his companion got up, stretched, sat down on the edge of the bed, then got up again.

"Tell me about Stuttgart," Cypher said five minutes after he had administered the injection. He was across the room looking down at the people snaking along Grafton Street like a conga line. College students dressed in flannel shirts and jeans made up the majority of pedestrians jamming the sidewalks, creating kaleidoscopic tides of color that ebbed and flowed to the dictate of crossing lights.

Palmer hesitated before answering. "It went as planned, but there was someone else there."

Cypher turned from the window. "Oh?"

"A warrior."

"CIA?"

"Much better. This one was as good as I've seen."

"You sound concerned. But it doesn't affect our plan now, does it?" He paused, staring unseeing into the distance. "In fact, it may indicate our communiqué has found its way to important people. People who would have access to covert groups outside the normal scope of government. The exact people we want to reach. His being there is a good sign."

"It was unexpected. That's all."

"But you're sure all three are dead—and that Reegan had the scarf and pistol."

"The new guy could have killed them all without my help," Palmer said with a nod.

"But you made sure that none of them was questioned." Cypher moved to the side of the bed, where he gazed at Adams's face for a moment before tenderly brushing aside a few strands of hair that had fallen over her forehead.

She stirred and moaned weakly.

"It's almost time." His voice was tremulous with excitement. "Our next task is to get the strontium. When are you going to Georgia?"

"Tonight. As soon as we're finished here. If my equipment is ready in Tbilisi, I should be able to reach the generator by 2:00 a.m."

"Good." Cypher ran his tongue over dry lips. "The nurse in the E.R. She's one of our new ones. After tonight, she'll be a liability."

"I'll take care of her when I return."

"Okay. Once you get the strontium, we'll be able to plan our attack. You seem edgy. Are you worried about the man in Stuttgart showing up again?"

Palmer shook his head. "No. He and I will meet again if it's meant to be. What you sense is that I simply don't share your overall confidence. Making the CIA believe the Order is behind the agent killings is one thing. Manipulating them into attacking our enemies is quite another."

Cypher settled himself onto the bed next to Adams. In a voice laced with impatience, he answered, "Can't you see the forces of history at work here? America is in the midst of an antiterrorist feeding frenzy. Once they believe that the North is behind the attacks on their country, they'll react as they did with the Taliban and wipe the Orange Order off the face of the Earth! And they won't stop there. In both Afghanistan and Iraq, the Americans disbanded the entire government that harbored the terrorists. They'll do the same up North."

He paused before continuing in a trembling voice, "From the day I learned that Katherine Adams had been assigned to the White House, I knew we were being selected. You and I are chosen," he said, blinking suddenly teary eyes, "to reunite Ireland! This woman will give us the details we need to plan our attack. My sources tell me that she's the one in charge of planning trips for the President and his cabinet. Depending on where you think you can deliver the bomb, we'll select one of those trips."

"I can put it anywhere public."

Cypher felt a shortness of breath, accompanied by the familiar dull throb that preceded an onslaught of pain. He reached into his shirt pocket, pinched up two loose pills and popped them into his mouth.

"Headaches," he answered his companion's raised eyebrow as he dry-swallowed the pills and turned his attention to Adams.

"Katey. Katey Adams," he spoke gently. "Can you hear me?"

"Um. Where am I?" Her speech was slurred.

"Tell me your social-security number."

"Nine-two-eight, four-six, four-five-four-one." The numbers were spoken in syncopation.

Cypher took a pad and pen from his jacket pocket.

"Katey, what are your duties at the White House?"

"Schedule trips… Draw up itineraries… Brief the Secret Service… Coordinate trips."

Cypher turned to Palmer, who was pulling the chair from the desk closer to the bed. "It's working. She'd never tell us that willingly." He leaned forward and spoke slowly. "Katey, where will the President be on August 17?"

There was a slight pause. "Camp David."

"No way," Palmer said. "Not enough time to get inside security like that."

"Not enough people," Cypher added. "We want something messy."

"Katey," he asked, "where will Margaret Moore be on August 17?"

"New Hampshire."

He arched his eyebrows and began writing.

"Where in New Hampshire?"

"Manchester and Concord. Six stops."

"Maybe," Palmer said. "I wonder how big the crowds will be."

"Maybe," Cypher agreed. He turned back to Adams. "Where will Daniel Foley be on August 17?"

"West Point," Adams answered.

Cypher clenched his fist and turned to face his partner. "Is there any doubt that God is on our side?" he asked. "West Point is perfect. The secretary of defense, whose family comes from Killarney. The place will be crawling with tourists. A terrorist attack on their military shrine will produce an all-out response from the Pentagon."

Directing his attention back to Adams, he asked, "Who is in charge of planning Foley's West Point trip?"

"I am."

The two men stared at each other as if unable to believe their good fortune. Palmer was the first to speak and, when he did, he cut right to the details.

"Katey, what is the secretary's itinerary for that day?"

There was a long pause as if she was awakening from a dream. A mental switch somewhere deep in her cortex was thrown and she began speaking in a monotone.

"Breakfast 0610…cadet seminars in Thayer Hall…lunch

with the corps...parade on the Plain...chopper to Camp Buckner...tour training, chopper to Kennedy...arrive Dulles by 1930."

"What do you think?" Cypher asked.

"I've done harder. We'll drop the bomb on him and the cadets during the parade," Palmer said.

"Just like that, you've decided? You don't need more information?"

"Goddamn you," he said in a suddenly harsh voice. "Don't insult me. Nothing I do is 'just like that.' You often forget that I, too, am a professional."

He paused to take a deep breath and, in a calmer voice said, "I've been there. Half a dozen times. The parade ground is wide-open on all sides except the front, where the point extends into the Hudson. From the rear and sides, the corps will be vulnerable. And the way granite absorbs radiation makes the place ideal for a dirty bomb. The mess hall and barracks surrounding the Plain will be contaminated for years!"

Cypher smiled a tight smile. "Good. You said during the parade. Means of delivery?"

"I don't know yet," Palmer replied, staring into the distance. "The more removed I can be, the better. Something with remote detonation. I don't know yet."

Cypher was about to say something when he was seized with a fit of coughing. Holding up his arm to ward his companion away, he hacked for a full minute, spitting up little globs of dark phlegm.

When the coughing finally subsided, he said in a whisper, "West Point. The next 9/11."

Thick fog filled the lowlands, reducing Palmer's visibility to what he could see in the vibrating halo cast by his powerful motorcycle's headlight. Although the highway out of Tbilisi was one of Georgia's major freeways, there had been almost no traffic for close to an hour as he sped west away from the city.

His objective was a defunct radiothermal generator, one of eighty-five deployed by the Soviets in the sixties and seventies in a string stretching from the Sea of Azov to Batumi on the Turkish border. For more than twenty years, the installations provided unmanned power for navigational beacons while also bringing rudimentary electricity to an area often isolated in winter by heavy storms. Forty years later, none of the RTGs were operational and had become liabilities of the new governments spun off from the Soviet Empire.

Although most sites had been secured under direction from the United Nations' International Atomic Energy Agency until its scientists decided what to do with the flashlight-sized lead canisters containing anywhere from ten to three hundred curies of strontium 90, very few locations were well defended. The radioactive fuel in the cells was not weapons grade and could not be enriched to become so. The new governments simply had more important issues on their agendas than protecting the old generators.

The outpost west of Senaki was one of the better-fortified installations, guarded by a platoon of thirty-four Georgian land troops. But, in spite of its defenses, Cypher had chosen Senaki's RTG for three reasons. First, there were two extra canisters from other sites in storage there. Second, the area's infrastructure had good highways and a spur of the national railroad running straight from Senaki to the port of Poti where trusted passage on a cargo ship bound for LeHavre had already been purchased. And, third, because he had full confidence in his assassin's talents.

For the type of dirty bomb Cypher envisioned, one canister containing at least fifty curies of strontium was all he needed.

As Palmer sped through the fog, wispy and patchy as his elevation increased, he recalled the schematics he had memorized before leaving Ireland. It was possible that the canisters would still be housed in the thousand-pound generators of their original RTGs, which would mean disassembling the power modules in order to reach the fuel packs.

A few years earlier, European newspapers had been filled with the story of three woodchoppers who'd come across a damaged canister up in the northwestern region of Abkhazia and had brought it back to their camp. No one knew how the fuel cell had gotten out into the middle of the remote forest to begin with, but two of the unfortunate men were dead. The third had ended up in a Paris hospital, suffering from a lethal dose of radiation poisoning.

Palmer had no intention of following their example. If the RTGs had to be disassembled, he was prepared to do it without damaging the casings. He glanced at his watch containing the built-in Geiger counter he would need once he reached the site.

Across his back, slung the way Apache warriors carried their bows enroute to battle, was an American XM-8 compact carbine in a black canvas travel bag. The 5.56 mm weapon was one of the U.S. Army's newest models.

Strapped to the outside of both his shins were Victorinox ten-inch throwing knives forged in Geneva by the same company that made the original Swiss Army knife. Beneath his Italian leather jacket, in a quick-draw holster, he carried a Walther PPK, its stubby sound suppressor designed to prevent the pistol from getting hung up if, in fact, he found himself in a situation actually requiring a quick draw. In his jacket pockets, he held two V-40 grenades.

The road became noticeably better as Palmer neared his destination, reflecting the republic's decision to start rebuilding its infrastructure close to the sea where tourists would come. Ten kilometers from the RTG site, the highway was smooth and wide, a modern thoroughfare ready and waiting for the international trade the Georgian government had promised during elections.

Close to his objective, he began to chant. The mantra's familiar words immediately elevated his mind to battle-ready status, honing his concentration to a razor's edge.

It was a few minutes after midnight when the paved road leading into dense woods cordoned off by a heavy chain-link fence appeared on his right. Two soldiers were on duty at a manual crossbar blocking the way. They were relaxed and smoking cigarettes.

When the motorcycle slowed to a stop in front of their position and the rider dismounted and walked toward them carrying what looked like a map, they discarded their smokes and straightened their caps.

"Hello," was all Palmer said, but it was enough to identify him as a British visitor.

"Hello. Stop, please, you are at a forbidden place," one of them replied haltingly, indicating his discomfort with English.

The soldiers drew close to each other as they took a few steps forward, apparently not noticing that the stranger's right hand had slipped inside his leather jacket. He strode purposely toward them, smiling amicably. Less than ten yards away, the man who had spoken opened his mouth to say something else, but his words were cut short by a silenced .38 ACP round that splattered portions of his frontal lobe out the back of his head. He toppled over like a prizefighter catching the wrong end of a roundhouse, eyes wide and unseeing.

His partner's face registered a millisecond of astonishment at the sudden appearance of the PPK before a matching slug drilled into the center of his forehead. A scarlet geyser immediately erupted from the neat hole. Arms flailing, he shimmied to the ground.

Palmer slid his pistol into its holster and moved quickly, grabbing a fistful of uniform in each hand so he could drag both bodies into the woods beyond the chain-link fence. They were lighter than the barbells he regularly trained with, posing no physical challenge as he hastily pulled them into the thick bushes a few yards off the road. Once his victims were hidden, he returned and walked his motorcycle to a spot behind a thick oak where he'd have easy access back onto the highway.

Before leaving his bike, he removed the XM-8 carbine from its carrying case and, from under the motorcycle's seat, grabbed a leather saddlebag stitched with three individual lead-lined compartments designed to hold the strontium canisters. Slinging the bag over his shoulder, he started up the road.

Palmer stayed on the pavement, partly to avoid trip wires that may have been rigged in the woods, but more to speed his approach. He knew the odds that the site was protected by booby traps or anything more than the troops assigned there were actually quite slim.

When he came to within fifty yards of the site, and the lighting in the compound cast its corona into the woods, Palmer left the pavement and slipped back between the trees. As silent as a phantom, he drew closer, dropping to one knee when he reached the coppice edge, where he placed the lead-lined saddlebag on the ground.

There were three buildings in a tight circle, illuminated by half a dozen spotlights mounted at the top of utility poles. A square windowless structure was obviously the oldest. From satellite pictures he had downloaded, Palmer knew that the single metal door he could see at the northwest junction of the concrete building's two sides was the workshop's only egress. Caution signs posted on the rust-streaked metal door displaying the international symbol for radioactive material left no doubt that this was where the radiothermal generator was housed.

Twenty yards from the RTG building stood the barracks, a relatively new wood-frame edifice twice as long as it was wide. There were doors on each end and, on the long side, eight evenly spaced windows. At the short end, farthest from Palmer's vantage point, a radio tower rose to a height of fifty yards.

Two military-style jeeps, a few fifty-five-gallon drums and a large tank with the word *Petrol* in red letters told him that the third building was the motor pool and utility shop. A rough humming emanating from inside the corrugated metal walls pinpointed the location of the generator providing power to the outside lights and buildings.

As Palmer continued his visual reconnaissance, two soldiers with AK-47s slung behind their shoulders came into view around a corner of the RTG building. He watched as they walked the length of the concrete wall, then turned to amble along the adjoining side, chatting casually. Palmer remained in place until the guards completed an entire lap, rounding the far corner a few minutes later. They appeared to be the only patrol and would therefore be his next targets.

Chanting his mantra anew, he visualized his attack. It was important that he take out the radio station before a distress call could be sent but, prior to approaching the barracks, he'd also have to make sure there was no one inside the motor pool who could engage. A platoon, he knew, consisted of thirty-four soldiers. Two were concealed in the woods down by the highway and two were on open patrol, which meant he'd be facing thirty opponents when he attacked.

After touch-checking the 36-round magazine locked and loaded into his XM-8, Palmer slung the saddlebag over his shoulder and began his approach. Moving lithely through the trees, he was rendered almost invisible in his black leather clothing. By remaining on the outer boundary of the soft halo of light touching the woods, he became nothing more than a flitting shadow as he stalked the two guards, his entire being as focused as that of a cheetah on the hunt.

When he reached the far side of the compound, he propped his assault rifle against a tree, placed the saddlebag on the ground and waited behind a sparse bush for the guards to make their appearance. They passed within ten yards of his spot, the tedium of the night having stripped them of any alertness they may have possessed at the outset of their detail.

Palmer let them pass before emerging from his position, while drawing both knives from their shin scabbards. Bringing his hands above and behind his head, he took a step forward and let the knives fly. They reached their marks within a nanosecond of each other, slicing cleanly through the olive-drab uniforms between the fifth and sixth ribs before piercing the young men's hearts. The soldiers grunted as they fell forward, dark stains spreading quickly across the back of their shirts where the knives protruded, buried in flesh up to the hilts. Palmer ran forward to his victims, finding that one was still alive and struggling to reach the trigger housing of his slung weapon, apparently to sound an alarm with his last iota of energy.

Palmer pulled the knife from the surviving soldier's back and, without hesitation, plunged it into the young man's neck at the base of his skull. All movement instantly stopped, the razor-sharp edge severing the link between brain stem and spinal cord.

As he had done earlier, he dragged the bodies into the woods, first retrieving and sheathing his knives. He then picked up and slung his carbine. Tossing the saddlebag into the shadow of the generator building where he could grab it up on the way in, he moved in a crouch toward the motor pool.

There was a single window on the far side of the building away from the compound. Through it, Palmer could see four soldiers at a small table in the middle of the room. They were playing cards while sharing a fifth of vodka that sat half empty on the table between them. The air immediately above was hazy with cigarette smoke. The room's perimeter was cluttered with workbenches containing an assortment of hand tools, engine hoses and fan belts. Numerous machine parts in various states of disassembly and repair sat haphazardly throughout, creating the impression that nothing was finished before a new task was undertaken.

The compound's generator sat at the far end of the building, purring loudly enough to cover the sounds the thirty-six 5.56 mm rounds loaded into the XM-8's clip were about to make. Arranged inside the magazine in two spring-tensioned parallel rows, the steel-jacketed bullets stood like paratroopers along the fuselage of a C-130, waiting for the green light.

Palmer pulled back from the window and walked quickly to the door. With the XM-8 cradled in his right arm, he turned the doorknob and entered, taking two steps inside before the soldiers looked up and realized he was not one of their own. Before the men could react, he began hosing the area with lethal slugs. The vodka bottle shattered as wood, flesh, blood and gore splattered and splashed in all directions. The soldiers twitched and danced like marionettes controlled by a mad puppeteer as the hot lead cut through their bodies.

The acrid smell of cordite quickly filled the motor pool, competing with the odor of sizzling blood and flesh. By the time the last round was fired and the rifle's bolt finally clicked open onto an empty chamber, the pile of tattered bodies strewed amid the blood-soaked remnants of the table and chairs resembled a restaurant hit scene from New York's Mafia wars.

Palmer jammed a fresh magazine into his XM-8's ammo port, chambered the first round and exited the motor pool, pulling the door closed behind him.

The barracks building had a door in the middle of each short side. Palmer ran through the woods to the end where the radio tower's cable snaked through a hole drilled at floor level, reaching into his jacket pocket for the two apple-sized grenades he had brought. They were V-40 fragmentation models, composed of a steel body with 326 individual squares pressed into the inside face, each of which became a separate piece of shrapnel when the explosive detonated. For the job immediately at hand, a percussion type grenade with a variable fuse would have been a better choice for disabling the transmitter, but, over the years, Palmer had developed a knack for making do with the equipment he had.

Reaching the door, he saw that the hinges were on the right side and that the door opened outward. The configuration meant that his toss would be left-handed, which, for someone who had been completely ambidextrous since early youth, was simply a matter of technique rather than difficulty. Cradling the two grenades in the palm of his left hand, he pulled the pins and, in one fluid motion, opened the door, tossed the grenades toward the radio and closed the door before anyone within had a chance to react.

In the three seconds before the explosions, the fleeting view Palmer had gotten of the barracks' interior flashed through his mind. There were sixteen bunk beds on each side, with three separate groups of soldiers assembled around beds on which they may have had tiny televisions or DVD players. One man sat at the radio and two or three solitary soldiers were in their bunks reading.

The grenades detonated with two simultaneous eardrum-throbbing concussions that exploded the windows outward in a hurricane of glass. A heartbeat later, Palmer burst through the door, his eyes searching for movement as the cries of the wounded reached his ears and the stink of death filled his nostrils. Bed linens were ripped and bloody, torn to pieces by the deadly shrapnel. Bodies littered the floor, cast into grotesque death poses by the explosions' unbridled force. Halfway down the room, a stunned soldier in a top bunk groped for a weapon hanging by its sling from the bedpost. Palmer stroked the XM-8's trigger, sending a short burst into the man's torso. He flew backward like a rag doll, bouncing off the wall where his body left a runny imprint resembling a Rorschach inkblot.

There was movement farther down from the other row of bunks and, again, the carbine's barrel spit death in a sharp staccato voice. On both sides of the center aisle, wounded soldiers moaned and writhed. Palmer engaged them with brief bursts, the 5.56 mm rounds whining and sparking in ricochets off the bunks' metal frames. Within ten seconds, the 36-round magazine was spent, and Palmer ejected it while reaching into his pocket for a fresh one. As he rammed it home, he could see from the corner of his eye that the radio operator was slumped facedown over his station, his uniform a bloody mess of shredded cloth and flesh.

With a fresh magazine loaded, Palmer walked down the middle of the barracks, counting the dead as he fired single shots into anyone who moved. When he reached the far door, he had killed nineteen, bringing his total for the night to twenty-seven.

A normal platoon was staffed with thirty-four soldiers. At any given time, some of them could be on leave, or the platoon could be deployed light, but as Palmer reached for the doorknob, pausing for a few final moments to empty his magazine into the radio transmitter at the other end of the barracks, the discrepancy in the number of soldiers nagged at his mind.

Once outside, he proceeded quickly to the RTG building where he retrieved his saddlebag. Finding the door with the radiation signs unlocked, he hurriedly entered, saddlebag across his shoulder, fully loaded XM-8 at the ready.

There was no one inside the single room, one-third of which was cordoned off by heavy metal screening plastered with radiation signs and symbols. A sliding door made of the same tightly woven chain link provided access into the generator area. As he approached the screen, Palmer could see a fully assembled unit and, on the floor next to it, two additional fuel canisters.

Lowering his weapon, he activated his wristwatch Geiger counter. It beeped slowly and steadily, detecting no errant radiation. The sliding door screeched as he pushed it aside on its metal runners, making a noise reminiscent of fingernails scratching a blackboard.

As he was loading the two extra fuel canisters into his saddlebag, Palmer swept over and across them with his watch, ensuring there were no pinpoint leaks in the lead casings. Once they were stored safely in the saddlebag's lead-lined compartments, he turned his attention to the generator.

Considering the unit's age, it was in remarkably good shape, the exterior casings displaying no signs of radiation leaks. The Soviet design had been a good one, with most generators functioning reliably for almost thirty years before electronic components finally gave out. As he removed the front panels, Palmer could tell from the original seals, now yellowed and brittle, that this particular generator had never undergone repair.

The third fuel canister was directly behind the RTG's power assembly. Palmer unlatched the power couplings, disconnected the sensor circuitry and, after a final check for radiation with his wristwatch Geiger counter, pulled the lead canister from its housing. Only when he had the fuel cell safely in his hands did he realize he had been holding his breath during the last step of disassembly when an overlooked coupling could have resulted in a dangerous release.

Displaying the gentleness of an obstetrics nurse cradling a new life, Palmer placed the third canister into the saddlebag before hefting it onto his shoulder. With its lead lining and full load of three fuel cells, the bag weighed close to one hundred pounds but, for someone who could bench press more than three hundred, or run ten miles while carrying weapons and a fully loaded combat pack, the weight was nothing more than an inconvenience.

He was on his way out, halfway across the open area to the woods, when he heard the jeep. A lack of headlights shining through the trees told him its occupants had to have found the absence of guards at the bottom of the road suspicious, which meant he would not have the element of surprise on his side when he engaged this new contingent.

Before another thought crossed his mind, the stutter of automatic fire filled the air and he was knocked off his feet as a round slammed into the lead-lined saddlebag slung across the front of his chest.

When Adams awoke from her tormented sleep for the third time, Mack Bolan was sitting in a chair next to the door, reading a paperback by the light spilling in from the hallway.

"Hey," she said.

He looked up from the book. "Hey."

"I thought you were in Stuttgart," she said while pushing herself onto one elbow, careful not to dislodge the intravenous tube secured to the back of her left hand with two intersecting strips of white surgical tape.

"I was told you needed protection. Flight time was less than two hours."

She nodded slightly, then glanced at the clock in the corner of the room, its red block numbers displaying 2:58 a.m.

"How long have you been here?"

"About an hour. How are you feeling?"

She lay her head back onto the pillow, turning to face the wall. "Nightmares, disorientation, terrible headache." She paused, swallowed hard and added, "I'm also kind of depressed…feeling big-time guilty."

"Truth serum."

"Yeah. You'd think knowing all the symptoms would make it easier. But it doesn't."

"There's no reason to feel guilty. The drug breaks everyone. Memory gaps and guilt are part of it." He paused. "Are you up for telling me what happened?"

Adams blew a long exhale through puffed cheeks before speaking.

"I was coming out of the shower in my hotel room, and someone grabbed me from behind and held a cloth soaked in what must have been chloroform against my face. That's all I remember."

"How did you get here? I read your chart and, from the way they reacted in the E.R., it's almost as if they were expecting you. Quick diagnosis, exactly the right treatment—it couldn't have been better."

"Bryan McGuinness came to my hotel to take me out to dinner. He was here when I woke up the first time. He said when I didn't answer his calls from the lobby, he convinced security to let him into my room. They found me unconscious and dialed 9-9-9."

"That's when you called Brognola? When you woke up the first time, I mean?"

"Yeah."

"And your friend was here with you."

"Yeah."

Bolan was staring into the distance, a frown on his face.

"It must be connected to the communiqué," Adams said, her words beginning to slur as she fought off the next round of sleep. "They knew I was back, and maybe they, um, maybe they—" she paused to yawn "—maybe they wanted to see how much progress we were making."

She glanced his way through heavy eyelids. "What? You don't think that's it?"

"They could have gauged our progress by watching where we went," Bolan answered with a quick shake of his head.

"The risk doesn't justify the results if all they wanted was a status report."

There was a soft knock on the door, more to announce than to request entry. A nurse came in and walked around the bed to the IV stand on the far side. She looked young—mid- to late-twenties, Bolan thought.

"You're awake," she said, checking the half-empty intravenous bag. "Are you feeling better?"

Adams made a murmuring sound, closed her eyes and drifted off to sleep.

"That's normal," the nurse said to Bolan while moving down the side of the bed to reach the medical chart hanging from a hook attached to the footboard's metal frame. She motioned with her head to the IV. "We have her on a Percocet drip. She'll drift in and out for the rest of the day."

"Nurse—" Bolan leaned forward to read her name tag "—Grylie. You were in the emergency room when Katey was brought in."

She seemed to freeze for an instant, an ever-so-slight hesitation that Bolan noted before adding, "I read her chart and saw that you signed the admitting paperwork. You're working a long shift."

"We were shorthanded last night," she said in a rush of words while making an entry into the chart. "So I was extended a bit. Just going off now, in fact."

She put the chart back onto its hook and turned to leave.

Bolan stepped in front of her.

"I saw, when I read the chart, that you started the Percocet and saline drip as soon as she got here. How did you know what the right treatment was before you saw the results of her blood test?"

Grylie's eyes darted to a spot high and to the right of Bolan. She ran her tongue quickly over her lips and, squinting slightly, said, "We thought someone had given her Rohypnol—the date-rape drug. That's what we started treating her for. I suppose you could say that luck was on our side. The doctor says whatever she took is in the same family."

"I'm impressed by how quickly you diagnosed her."

"It's what we do in Emergency, Mr..."

"Cooper. I'm a colleague."

Avoiding his gaze, Nurse Grylie stepped around Bolan to leave. "It was nice meeting you, sir. Don't worry about your friend. She'll be released today."

Once the nurse was gone, Bolan went to the rocking chair by the window. Despite the hospital being in the center of a city, it was quiet on the street below. Unlike New York or Los Angeles, Dublin actually slept at night.

Nurse Grylie suddenly appeared on the sidewalk, heading north at a brisk pace. Bolan surmised her destination was probably the DART station a few blocks over on Pearse Street, where the Dublin Area Rapid Transit ran commuter trains to the suburbs 24/7. She glanced once over her shoulder, directly at Bolan as if she could feel him watching, before she turned at the corner and disappeared.

As Bolan rocked slowly, his mind churned. He was sure that the unseen gunman in Stuttgart, the one armed with a sniper rifle, had been there to make certain that none of Randolph's attackers survived. In Dublin, someone had been waiting for the CIA to send Adams. The attack in her hotel and the quick treatment in the E.R. were too perfect not to have been set up in advance.

The situation was being manipulated, that much was clear. But, by whom and for what purpose eluded Bolan.

He continued to rock, dozing fitfully as the minutes turned to hours while his subconscious wrestled to match motives with actions.

Knocked off his feet by a round that slammed into the lead-lined saddlebag slung across his chest, Palmer immediately went into a roll and scramble, going into a prone position behind one of the telephone poles supporting the spotlights that illuminated the compound. Dust kicked up in a little cloud from the hard-packed earth when he landed, filling his nostrils with an acrid smell of burned motor oil. Ignoring an urge to sneeze, he hugged the ground to make his profile as small as possible.

Peering out from behind the cover of the three-foot-high concrete base, he trained his XM-8 in the direction of the incoming rounds. Muzzle-flashes flared from two locations among the trees alongside the road as lethal lead snapped through the air a finger's width above his head.

From the intersection where concrete met earth, he began to return fire in 3-round bursts. His enemies were probably behind trees and safe from being hit, but at least his volleys would keep them pinned down while he planned his next move.

Palmer reasoned that his attackers were probably the missing soldiers in the platoon and, until he was able to scour the area to his satisfaction, he would proceed with the assumption that seven was the number he was facing. As if to confirm his thoughts, gunfire erupted from the other side of the road leading into the site. There were at least five.

As the soldiers fired, Palmer took note of their general locations before aiming six shots in quick succession at the spotlights mounted on top of the poles, shattering them in a shower of sparks and glass shards that plunged the compound into absolute darkness.

The sudden blackness produced the desired effect, surprising his less-experienced adversaries by imposing an unexpected situation upon them. They immediately stopped shooting and began calling softly to one another. As Palmer raised himself into a crouch in preparation for his dash to another spot, he could hear their voices whispering back and forth across the road.

The Geiger counter in his wristwatch began to chirp, indicating that one of the fuel canisters was leaking strontium. He left the saddlebag behind the concrete base and raced off toward the woods to his right, the cover of darkness shielding him from sight.

As he neared the edge, a voice called out loudly, shouting a few sentences in Russian. After pausing for a few seconds, the same voice yelled, "Hello! Surrender! We are outnumbering you. Throw down your guns and we will not kill you."

As if to reinforce their weapons superiority, the troops began firing in the direction of the light pole where Palmer had been.

As their rounds tore up the earth around the pole's concrete base, Palmer sprinted through the woods until he was twenty yards behind the soldiers. Turning left, he circled in for the kill.

An illumination flare's ignition cap sounded, followed within seconds by another. Palmer threw himself to the ground behind a tree.

The white phosphorous flares ignited, bathing the compound in bright flickering light as they floated slowly toward the ground under tiny silk parachutes. The harsh glare cast the night into extreme contrast, creating a surreal study in black and white.

Moving very slowly, Palmer peeked around the side of the tree. Two soldiers were slightly off to his right, in prone positions behind a fallen log. Their attention was focused on the compound, making their exposed backs easy targets under the illumination from the flares. But they were only two of seven, and Palmer knew it was important to keep his position concealed from the others for as long as possible.

Knowing that the slightest move could draw the eye of anyone who happened to be looking his way, he inched his hand under his jacket to draw the Walther. The flares expired. All was dark, but he knew exactly were his enemies were and he was able to take careful aim as he rose to his full height. Holding his carbine in his left hand, he squeezed off four quick shots from the pistol in his right, the muffled cough of the PPK's silenced rounds swallowed by the surrounding trees.

The soldiers cried out, scrambling madly to turn. They began firing their weapons wildly in his direction, shattering the night air with eardrum-pulsing chatter.

Flak jackets, Palmer thought, dropping his Walther so he could bring the XM-8 carbine to bear while throwing himself to the side, away from their line of fire. Even before he hit the ground, he was hosing the area to the front with a steady stream of 5.56 mm slugs that tore into the soldiers torsos below the protection of their Kevlar vests. Steel-jacketed NATO rounds shattered hips and pelvises, slicing men almost in two at the waist, hammering their lifeless bodies onto the forest floor.

Palmer's bolt clicked open onto an empty chamber. His left hand ejected the spent magazine while, a millisecond later, his right one inserted a fresh cartridge holding thirty-six rounds.

Three flares popped in quick succession as the dead soldiers' comrades decided to illuminate the area before entering the melee where, in the darkness, they could end up firing at their buddies.

When he heard the first ignition pop, Palmer began to run, intending to put as much distance as possible between himself and the two he had just killed. He was ticking off the fuse delay in his head and hit the ground an instant before the first flare ignited. The second came right after, then the third, and the woods were bathed once more in eerie light.

Palmer had landed in a patch of waist-high bushes that concealed him well, but afforded almost no cover. Peering through the branches with one eye, he watched for movement.

At first, there was none. His adversaries were taking the same approach—remaining motionless, waiting for something to draw their eyes. It was the proper tactic for this situation, but it required patience and steel-willed discipline. Under the flickering light of flares that illuminated a landscape where a bloodthirsty monster lurked, Palmer knew it was easy for young soldiers to get spooked. Especially when their hearts were pumping four times the normal amount of adrenaline through their systems.

Something real or imaginary caught the attention of one of the soldiers, and he opened fire, spraying the woods at the edge of the compound in full-auto mode. He was joined by another, the flashes from the end of their barrels close together, fifty yards from where Palmer lay.

They were, apparently, under the impression that he was

still coming from the direction of the compound. A surprise assault from the rear was possible, but it would have to be done in a way that would not alert the remaining men to his location.

The flares went out, and he jumped to his feet and began to run toward his enemies. His closed eye had retained enough night vision for him to avoid crashing into trees and he closed the distance quickly. When the first of three pops sounded, announcing that the next round of flares was airborne, he calculated that he was within ten yards of his prey.

He threw himself forward, landing in a mossy area behind a rotting log. The flares ignited a second later, and he saw that his estimate had been accurate. Less than ten yards away, two soldiers armed with AK-47s were in perfect kneeling positions. One was a lefty, and they were leaning into both sides of the same tree trunk for stability. Unfortunately for them, they were facing away, their attention focused on the compound.

Unlike the .38 rounds from the Walther, the XM-8's 5.56 mm slugs would easily penetrate Kevlar at this range. But, without knowing where the remaining three soldiers were, engaging these two in a firefight would be a risky proposition.

Pushing his carbine a few inches away, Palmer reached down to his shin scabbards, drawing the ten-inch throwing knives. With one in each hand, he visualized his attack while the light from the flares gave him the opportunity to fix in his mind the proximity of the soldiers to one another, as well as their exact distance from his spot.

One of the other three called out, perhaps asking if the intruder could be seen, and someone yelled back a response without budging an inch.

The first flare went out, and Palmer drew one leg up under

him in a pose similar to that of a sprinter in the blocks, ready to surge forward at the sound of the starter's pistol.

The two remaining flares went out, and he exploded forward, closing the distance before the soldiers had time to comprehend what the rushing sound behind them meant.

The man on the right turned, and Palmer thrust the knife into the area above the Kevlar vest, aiming for the man's neck. The forceful flood of warm blood that came gushing onto his hand, followed by panicked choking sounds as his enemy slid to the ground, told him he had found the jugular.

The soldier who fired lefty tried to jump away from the tree so he could bring the barrel of his rifle around to bear, but Palmer leaped onto him, throwing him onto his back. As he clamped his bloody right hand in a steel-like vise grip over the man's mouth, his left arm thrust ten inches of hardened steel up under the vest.

The smell of intestines filled the air as severed organs poured through the gaping wound onto Palmer's slick leather clothes before sliding to the moss-covered earth. The soldier struggled fervently for a few seconds, until the extreme loss of blood sapped his strength, and Palmer was able to withdraw the knife and plunge it into his victim's throat, killing him immediately.

Palmer rolled off the body, taking a few moments to wipe his bloody hands on the dead man's shirt.

Three remained. As he retrieved his fully loaded XM-8, Palmer considered a simple frontal assault. The compound's access road was a few yards off to his right. He hadn't crossed it yet, but he knew the final three were either with their jeep or across the asphalt on the other side.

Staying parallel to the tar, Palmer moved farther away from the compound until he guessed he was approximately fifty yards from the jeep. He thought at least one of the remaining soldiers would be with the vehicle, probably crouched behind the hood for cover, or, perhaps, beneath the chassis in a prone firing position.

As he walked, the terrorist reached into an inside pocket of his jacket and scooped up the five special tracers he had brought. Without breaking stride, he ejected the full magazine from his XM-8 and fingered out the top five bullets, replacing them with the tracers. After locking the magazine back into place and chambering the first round, he dropped to the ground and crawled to the edge of the road.

One of the soldiers called out to his dead companions. Receiving no reply, he fired off another white phosphorous flare. The jeep was illuminated, parked across the road as if to restrict traffic. One soldier was beneath the vehicle, as Palmer had expected, and, in the flickering light of the descending flare, another could be seen crouched by a tree on the far side of the road.

Palmer aimed his XM-8 at the spare gas tank mounted on the back of the jeep and waited for the flare to expire. At the instant the light went out, when the soldiers' eyes would begin readjusting to the darkness, he opened fire with the five multipurpose rounds.

Red tracers cut through the night.

The first incendiary slug found its mark, detonating the spare gas tank into a fireball that splashed burning gasoline across the road. The jeep's internal gas tank was hit by a subsequent round, which ignited it with a blast that lifted the vehicle's back tires off the ground and sent a shock wave through the woods that could be felt fifty yards away. Ragged shrapnel flew out in all directions.

The soldier under the jeep, stunned almost unconscious by the explosion, was set on fire by a spray of burning fuel. Roaring in pain, he pulled himself upright and staggered toward the edge of the woods, his uncertain step and windmilling arms giving him the look of a B-movie monster.

In the orange glow, Palmer sighted the stumbling soldier, and, firing the XM-8 on full-auto, stitched him with a short burst across the back of his torso. The impact of the slugs shoved him facedown, burning and bleeding, onto the road. His lifeless body hissed and popped as the gas-induced flames licked hungrily at his blood-soaked uniform, filling the night air with the stench of scorched flesh.

The soldier behind the trees was joined by his remaining comrade, and the two responded on full-auto, the chatter of their AK-47s competing against an increasing din of fire as flames spread into the dry woods.

Rounds tore up the ground around Palmer's position, sending clods of dirt into his face. He was in a shallow hollow, protected, for the most part, from their weapons, but he had no desire to prolong this standoff. Sighting as best he could at the muzzle-flashes, he stopped firing and waited.

The blazing woods on the far side of the road provided some illumination, improving target visibility. Palmer experienced a sense of déjà vu, patiently waiting for what he knew was already a foregone conclusion. The soldiers would either think they had killed him and come to investigate, or the fire would encroach on their position, forcing them to change location. Either way, the result would be the same. All he had to do was to wait them out.

Above the noise of the fire, a voice called out in English. "Hello! We are wanting a truce. Let us talk."

Palmer remained still, his eyes unblinking above the front sight of his XM-8.

"Hello! We will let you go, leave. We are not to stop you. Go!"

Seconds stretched into minutes with the only sound the

hissing and popping of dry wood as flames crept through the underbrush.

One of the soldiers dashed from his position to a spot behind the burning jeep. His companion sprinted to the edge of the trees, opening covering fire for his buddy to attempt a sprint from the jeep to the side of the road where their enemy lay.

With bullets slicing the air inches above him, Palmer squeezed one round from his XM-8, stopping the advancing soldier dead in his tracks before he took his third step.

The remaining soldier threw his weapon into the middle of the road and emerged with his hands held high above his head. Palmer ended his life with a prolonged burst that hammered the man back into the woods.

Palmer sprinted up the road past the carnage, past the telephone pole where he had left the saddlebag and into the generator building. There were half a dozen hazmat suits hanging from hooks on the wall, and he grabbed the largest. After removing one of his bloodstained throwing knives from its shin scabbard for use outside the protective suit, he pulled the one-piece unit on over his clothes. Grabbing the knife, he walked to the door, zipping the groin-to-neck zipper with his other hand as he went.

The Geiger counter on his watch began to chirp when he got close to the telephone pole, reminding him that this was a task demanding speed. He quickly found the saddlebag and, by passing his wristwatch over each of the three compartments, he was able to isolate the one holding the damaged canister. The knife's hardened steel, honed to a razor's edge, sliced through the lead-reinforced leather, severing the punctured compartment from the other two.

Palmer slung the intact saddlebag over his shoulder and ran

toward the road, leaving the leaking canister and his knife behind.

While jogging down the access road to his hidden motorcycle, he squirmed out of the protective suit and discarded it in the middle of the road.

Palmer placed the saddlebag into the compartment under the bike's seat, climbed aboard and thumbed the ignition. The engine immediately jumped to life, purring with restrained power as he eased onto the asphalt.

Traffic was nonexistent in the middle of the night on the Georgian Military Highway as he headed west. It was a full fifteen minutes before he passed another vehicle, a run-down pickup truck laden with hay lumbering toward the seaport town of Poti, whose lights could be seen in the distant sky.

Palmer plied the throttle and leaned into the wind as he sped past the pickup, enjoying the sudden rush of adrenaline the bike's quick acceleration produced.

"Two nights ago, at one of the old RTGs in Georgia," Akira Tokaido said. "Strontium 90. Word is, 150 curies were taken. There was a spill. The IAEA went in to clean up."

Mack Bolan looked from Akira Tokaido to Carmen Delahunt, Hal Brognola and Katey Adams. They were back in the War Room at Stony Man Farm, called together by Brognola.

"How bad was it?" Adams asked.

"Thirty-four dead," Brognola answered. "An entire infantry platoon. But not from the radiation."

In response to the woman's raised eyebrows, he continued, "Strontium is at the weak end of the radioactive spectrum. Limited exposure won't kill you. But it's perfect for a dirty bomb. Just like Akira said last week. A weapon of mass disruption."

Bolan recalled that the talented hacker had also said he'd start to troll the Internet, looking for clues that could tip them off to upcoming terrorist activities. Since then, the farm's bank of computers had processed billions of data items through filtering programs.

"So what killed them?" Adams asked.

Her toughness impressed Bolan. Forty-eight hours after enduring a chemical assault on her mind and body, she was as ready as the rest of them to throw herself back into the fray.

"Not what," Brognola said, "who?"

Bolan advanced the story to its logical conclusion. "Looks to me like a terrorist strike team went in, killed them all and stole the strontium."

Brognola's next words surprised the group. "Our contacts in-country say it was a single agent. There was only one set of intruder footprints at the site and all the rounds came from two weapons—an XM-8 and a PPK." He paused. "I know of only one man who could do something like that."

Delahunt and Tokaido turned to look at Bolan just as Aaron Kurtzman wheeled himself into the room. Huntington Wethers was right behind.

"Sorry we're late," Kurtzman said as he rolled to the place at the conference table left open for him. "Where are you?"

"Single agent," Brognola said.

"A Striker-type strike," Kurtzman said with a slight smile at his pun on Bolan's code name. "Have you discussed the scarf yet?"

Brognola turned back to the group. "An orange scarf was left inside the generator building. Another tag to make sure we know it was them."

Delahunt shifted in her chair. "The scarves bother me. I'm convinced it's the same group that sent the communiqué, but I'm not positive it's the Orange Order. I've been thinking about Striker's statement last week when he said that Oxford was undercover for more than a year, but the first time he mentioned Cypher was only three months ago. Where did this man, who is apparently calling the shots, come from?"

Kurtzman broke the pensive silence that followed the question by asking, "You're proposing that Cypher, himself, may be undercover from another organization?"

"I've said it from the start: anyone can plant a scarf. This group's brazenness doesn't sit well with me. The way they keep telling us they're a splinter group of the Order..." Her voice tapered off.

"I'm inclined to agree," Adams said, "that something's not right. While it's normal for a terrorist group to claim responsibility in order to force their agenda, here we have denials from the same organization. My contacts in the Order swear it's not them."

"Obviously, anyone can claim to be someone else," Kurtzman said slowly, "but why? The demands are exactly what the Order would want. They've been fighting for sovereignty for more than sixty years. If not them, then who?"

Wethers cleared his throat, and said, "We should be looking at this from the inside out. Who in Ireland benefits from a disruption in the status quo? Any disruption, regardless of whether the change, itself, is favorable on the surface to either side. Suppose it's not the North, and this group carries their plan to the final threat. What are the benefits for anyone—inside or outside of Ireland—of a terrorist attack on the United States?"

There were no responses.

Kurtzman spread his hands out in front of him on the table, and said, "What we must do, people, is corroborate the evidence. Have we established any independent links to the North?"

"No. Pointing us to the Order is what the perps left at the scenes," Delahunt said.

"Except for Bobbie Reegan," Adams said. "He's a verified link to the Order. Not a good one at anything like a policy level, but we know he was one of their thugs. He was carrying the Ruger that killed Johnston, Taylor and Buckley. And he had an orange scarf with him, apparently intending to leave it with Randolph's body."

"Reegan was set up in Stuttgart," Bolan said. "Did you read

the after-action report? A .357 slug, the same caliber Randolph uses. Made to look like an ambush, Randolph kills them all and, under normal circumstances, no one ever thinks to match the killer rounds with his weapon. Why would you? But I'm convinced the sniper was there to make sure none of those three walked away."

"Dead men tell no tales," Delahunt said.

"Exactly," Bolan agreed. "Reegan was a minor punk, easy to be played for a pawn." He paused for a moment, before saying, "We're all being manipulated. And not just in Stuttgart. Katey's nurse at the hospital in Dublin knew more than she was saying." He turned in his seat to face Adams. "That E.R. was waiting for you. It was all too perfect."

She nodded. "I wish we had something or someone with stronger ties to the North. Before the CIA can move forcibly, we have to establish irrefutable accountability."

To all present, there was no apparent rhyme or reason to the agent assassinations, Adams's drugging and the information obtained from Oxford's molar. Yet everyone assembled around the heavy conference table felt like they were witnessing the orchestrated opening gambits of a chess game where the stakes could very well be international instability.

"Where does that leave us?" Wethers finally asked, breaking the quiet.

"Akira and Carmen will continue trolling the Internet to see if we can pick up the strontium's trail," Kurtzman said. "It's important for us to find that stuff before it ends up in a dirty bomb. You and I, Hunt, will run some scenarios. Try to rough out motives and outcomes."

"I'll conduct a soft probe at the Order depot in Londonderry you guys found," Bolan said.

"We didn't exactly find it," Delahunt told him. "Anonymous tip, one more thing that makes me uneasy."

"I'm going with you," Adams said, her words carrying a challenging tone.

"Wait a minute," Brognola said. "I haven't heard anything about a probe."

"That's because it's classified," Bolan answered with a shrug. Everyone in the room knew that he was going forward regardless of authority or approvals.

Brognola stared hard at Bolan, the pulsing of the vein at his temple belying his otherwise calm demeanor.

After a few seconds, he asked in a resigned voice, "What do you need?"

"Aerials."

Kurtzman took a few big slugs of coffee, looking like a horse drinking water. "Okay," he said, pausing between gulps, "we can get those."

"Do you need tools?" Brognola asked.

"We're all set," Adams said, staring hard at Bolan. "I have contacts in-country."

"*Soft* probe," Brognola said, knowing that, with Bolan, *soft* was a very ambiguous adjective. "Minimal contact, right?"

Bolan nodded while staring into the distance, his jaw set in a straight, hard line.

"As minimal as possible," Adams replied, her words bringing the slight hint of a smile to the corners of Bolan's mouth.

11

From the outside, the bookstore called the Loft resembled its Dominick Street neighbors. To the left was a small hardware shop specializing in upscale reproductions, its window cases displaying an array of fancy hinges, doorknobs and latches cast in shiny brass and pewter. The shop's clientele was a new breed of young Irish professionals who were claiming Dublin's neglected neighborhoods.

To the right of the Loft was a store called Sigmas, which stocked expensive handbags, shoes and designer accessories. Its very existence in this section of Dublin was a testament to the economic revival of an area where unemployment had once been greater than twenty percent.

All three stores had undergone extensive renovations in the past two years, as had every other establishment in a three-block stretch on Dominick Street in what Dublin politicians liked to cite as a stellar example of urban redevelopment.

Two largely unknown characteristics differentiated the Loft from its neighbors. It had been operated by the same owner—a proprietor named Michael Shaughnessy—for more than twenty years. And, in a section of the basement accessible only through a hidden staircase in the owner's office, was what Katey Adams believed was the best-stocked weapons cache in southern Ireland.

In the harsh bare-bulb glare of the basement, Shaughnessy watched as Adams selected an Imbel .22-caliber pistol with mounted sound suppressor from the red velvet-lined tray on which his items were displayed like fine gems. Shaughnessy was a middle-aged man with an athlete's body, gone a little soft around the middle, but with broad shoulders, large hands and an explosive manner of movement.

"Come now, Katherine," he said with a twinkle in his eye. "A .22? A night out with the sisters, is it?"

"All-Ivy, Mikey. Why mess with success?"

"All-Ivy, my arse. Ten years ago, you win a county shoot here and, for the rest of our lives, we have to hear you're All-Ivy? Jesus Christ, a .22." He turned to Bolan. "I hope she shows a bit more maturity between the sheets, my friend."

"I wouldn't know," Bolan said while choosing a Spectre, the Italian submachine gun less than fourteen inches long with its stock folded, yet capable of feeding 9 mm bullets from a unique 50-round box magazine at a mind-numbing rate of 850 rpm.

"That's more like it!" Shaughnessy said. "You're better at choosing lovers than weapons, Katherine. He's one who knows stronger, faster, bigger! That's the fix, in bed or out!"

"Not your area of expertise from what I hear in the ladies' room," Adams said with a laugh.

She put down the Imbel and picked up a SIG-Sauer P-229 semiautomatic pistol.

"I love it when you're fresh," Shaughnessy replied.

"Ammo?" she asked.

"Standard and hollowpoint. All you want."

Adams leaned forward and picked up a pair of Crosman 972BV Black Venom tranquilizer pistols.

"Mother of God, Katherine. Have you no pride?"

"Screw you, Mikey. What's the range on these?"

He took one of the pistols from her, smiling fondly at the blued steel the way an antiques dealer might smile when handling a priceless artifact. "Fine pieces, indeed," he said, all business. "The grips have been hollowed out and retooled to accommodate two Copperhead 231B cartridges. Pump action plus CO_2, we're talking fifty meters, no degradation. I have Substance P darts that will drop a man dead in his tracks. Instantly. Out for an hour."

She took the pistols and placed them, along with Bolan's SMG and her SIG-Sauer, into the backpack they had brought with them.

"An hour," Shaughnessy repeated, "when you can have your way with him."

Ignoring his comment, she moved to a display case containing communications equipment.

For his secondary weapon, Bolan selected a Heckler & Koch MK-23 Automatic Colt Pistol with four 12-round magazines.

"I have ACP plus P," Shaughnessy said, referring to the enhanced ammunition the MK-23 had been designed to accommodate. The .45-caliber ACP+P cartridges were full-metal-jacketed 185-grain truncated cone slugs, which, due to the ammo's higher pressure and muzzle velocity, enabled greater accuracy than that achievable with standard .45 rounds.

"Do you have any Orvilles?"

Shaughnessy drew back at the question, eyeing his aloof customer in a new light.

Among covert groups operating outside the bounds of international laws and conventions, Orville was the nickname for a highly explosive round packing more punch than TNT, thus giving a .45-caliber bullet the destructive force of a small grenade.

"I have six."

"I'll take them."

"What's your comm preference?" Adams asked Bolan while he was putting the H&K handgun and magazines into their backpack.

"One-piece with throat mike," he said.

"Yeah. There's a pair here. I'm okay with that."

She added the comm gear, grappling equipment and night-vision goggles to their order while Shaughnessy retrieved ammunition and darts from a six-foot-high steel cabinet in the corner of the room.

"How are we paying today?" he asked as he placed magazines and boxes of ammo into the backpack. Bolan noticed that one of the magazines was sealed in clear plastic to keep the Orvilles in a moisture-controlled environment during storage.

"The account's still open," Adams answered, referring to a CIA account at the Irish National Bank to which Shaughnessy had access. Within a few days, he'd make a transfer, never considering, for even a moment, to overcharge one of his best customers.

Bolan shouldered the backpack, and they climbed the stairs to the office. At the shop's side door accessing an alleyway perpendicular to Dominick Street, Shaughnessy gave Adams a hug.

"God be with you," he said, holding her tight. "Be careful, Katherine."

To Bolan, he whispered while shaking hands, "Watch over her, now."

Bolan nodded, hitched the backpack a little higher onto his shoulder and followed Adams through the alley onto Dominick.

Morning showers had cleared, leaving Dublin smelling

clean and fresh. A strong July sun was chasing the remnant clouds, luring Trinity students from their summer studies to spend a few hours outdoors. Chatting and laughing, the young people passed Bolan and Adams, who'd opted to walk the dozen blocks to a CIA safehouse rather than take their hardware onto public transportation.

"How are you doing?" Adams asked after they had been walking for ten minutes, referring not only to the weight of the backpack but also to Bolan's silence since leaving Shaughnessy's.

"You don't have to come tonight."

"Neither of us has to. But we both will."

They lapsed back into silence for another five minutes until Adams said, "This way," while turning onto Kevin Street.

Halfway down the block, the safehouse was a middle apartment in one of the long row houses that lined both sides of the street. The unit was high for a ground-floor flat, with a steel, windowless front door at the top of a dozen redbrick stairs. As Adams unlocked the door by placing her thumb on an LCD pad above the heavy latch, she noticed Bolan staring at the beveled windowpanes.

"Bulletproof," she said, "and so heavily tinted not even infrared can see inside."

The door opened onto a front-to-back archway that divided the living space almost perfectly in two. To the left, Bolan could see into a bedroom suite he assumed had an attached bathroom. An eat-in kitchen and living room were on the right. Hardwood floors ran throughout the apartment, with a thick Persian rug covering all but a perimeter margin in the living room. The decor was high-end New York chic—black-and-white leather, accents in chrome and glass, granite countertops and stainless-steel appliances.

Bolan went into the bedroom where he dropped the backpack onto the bed while Adams checked their food supply in the kitchen.

"Plenty to eat," she said when he joined her a few minutes later. "Want something? There's cold cuts, pasta, all kinds of stuff."

"Whose place is this? The bathroom is full of candles and one of the shelves in the medicine cabinet is stocked with massage oils."

"Probably someone's love nest," she answered dismissively. "Do you want anything?" she asked again.

"Whatever you're having. I'll get our gear ready."

Bolan left the kitchen while Adams prepared pasta with tomato sauce from a can. He returned when the smell of food had permeated the apartment. He had changed into a lightweight black turtleneck and black pants and was carrying a stack of aerial photographs that he placed in two piles on the table next to their plates.

While they ate, they studied the pictures for, at least, the hundredth time, noting the number of guards, the weapons they carried and the times they made their rounds. When they finished, they felt as if they had actually walked the land—from the stand of trees next to the country road where they'd leave their car, across the fields partitioned by intersecting stone walls, to the farmhouse with the a detached barn where they hoped they'd find 150 curies of radioactive strontium.

THE IRISH COUNTRYSIDE WAS pitch black on a moonless night. Adams steered the Volvo off the road to a spot behind a clump of bushes where it would be hidden from passing motorists, although they hadn't seen anyone in either direction for more than ten miles. After switching off the engine, they sat silent for a few minutes, letting their eyes adjust to the total darkness.

"You know where we are?" Bolan asked.

"G6," she replied, referring to a grid on the photographs they had memorized. "North is straight ahead."

"Let's go. Watch for trip wires."

Adjusting their night-vision goggles to fit snugly against their eyes, they set off through the woods, using the high-stepping gait employed by U.S. Special Forces in Vietnam when they swept through an area suspected of being laced with booby traps. The exaggerated motion was strenuous and, by the time they reached the edge of the coppice, Adams and Bolan were sweating.

"Good," she whispered into her throat mike as each both dropped to one knee and scanned the open field leading to the farmhouse and barn. Ten yards in front of them, serving as the boundary between the field and woods, was one of the stone walls built from rocks and boulders that had been harvested every spring for centuries from the Irish soil. Keeping low, they dashed across the open space to a spot behind it.

"See anyone?" Bolan asked as he touch-checked the Spectre submachine gun. His H&K MK-23 was holstered at his left shoulder, a 12-round magazine locked and loaded with .45-caliber enhanced ammunition. In a quick-draw holster attached to his belt, he carried one of the Crosman 972 Black Venoms loaded with Substance P.

The tranquilizer belonged to a family of bioregulators that was closely related to compounds found naturally in the body. Substance P was developed in the late seventies by Soviet scientists to cause a rapid loss of blood pressure. Extremely effective, less than one microgram induced almost immediate unconsciousness.

"No," Adams answered, sweeping her eyes from left to right.

Her SIG-Sauer P-229 was slung low on her right hip, the way a gunfighter in the Wild West might have worn his weapon. Her Crosman 972BV was in a Kevlar shoulder holster strapped snugly across her chest.

They had rehearsed on paper with the photos so, when Bolan set off to circle the buildings, Adams knew exactly where he was going and where she was supposed to be. She angled her approach to be behind and to Bolan's right, stopping when she was about thirty yards from the barn. Through her goggles, she could see Bolan as he crept forward, moving slowly toward the building.

"Dog!" she said into the mike, and Bolan immediately stopped.

Right on schedule, the guard was upwind between her and Bolan, about fifteen yards from her spot. The man was holding a German shepherd dog at the end of a leash and the way the animal was straining to go forward indicated it had picked up Bolan's scent. The fact that it was not barking told Adams it was superbly trained, able to lead his handler to an intruder in silence.

Adams drew the loaded pistol from her shoulder holster and, as they had agreed while studying the photos, sighted in on the dog. Exhaling slowly to steady herself, she awaited Bolan's direction. The 972BV was a single shot weapon, which meant neither she nor Bolan would have a second chance to prevent an alarm from being sounded if they missed their targets.

"Ready." Bolan's voice sounded in her earplug. "Three… two…one…fire."

She squeezed the trigger and, two seconds later, the dog and his handler went down like sacks of grain.

"Clear," Adams said into her mike, and Bolan resumed his crouched approach.

When they came close to where a halo of light spilled out from inside the farmhouse, they stopped again.

"Guards. Two," Adams heard in her earplug a second before she saw them rounding the corner of the barn.

Again, as she and Bolan had agreed during rehearsals, Adams sighted her Crosman on the guard closest to the buildings.

"Ready. Three…two…one…fire."

The guards fell to the ground within a second of each other.

While Adams moved to her next position behind a waist-high privet hedge bordering a paved driveway where three SUVs were parked, Bolan ran to the back wall of the barn, pulling a small grappling hook with attached line from his belt pouch.

There were loft doors on both the front and back of the building, with thick beams to support hoists and pulleys extending straight out from the top of the door frames. Bolan tossed his line above the beam and pulled it taut for the hook to catch. With his Spectre SMG slung across his back, he began to walk up the side of the barn like a human fly. The boards were slippery and, more than once, his feet lost purchase, causing him to swing forward into the rough siding where he dangled precariously for a few seconds before steadying his motion. With the tendons on his forearms standing out like steel cables, he pulled himself, inch by inch, up the slender rope. When he finally reached the loft door, which was mounted on a rail like the sliding door on a railway boxcar, he pushed it to the right and stepped inside.

Adams stood to join Bolan, but, before she was able to take her first step in that direction, the farmhouse door opened, and she ducked back down where she could peer through the privet's branches. A man came out and crossed the porch to the stair railings, his arms reaching to the front and sides as if for balance. He called out a greeting with a thick tongue to an approaching guard and dog, who were a full five minutes ahead of schedule. His unsteady step as he teetered down the stairs, indicated he was more than slightly inebriated.

Adams drew the Crosman with her right hand while, with her left, she pulled a second dart from one of the six loops stitched into the holster.

The drunken man staggered to a spot not more than four feet from where she was hidden behind the hedge and unzipped his fly, the sound of the zipper seeming unreasonably loud against the pounding in her ears.

The guard with the dog came closer, and she heard him say, "Come on, boy, it's just John. Come on."

When the dog began growling with a low guttural sound that sent a shiver down her spine, Adams sprang to her feet with coiled-spring speed, the tranquilizer pistol extended straight out. She squeezed the trigger, then, with lightning precision, loaded the second dart as her mind registered two things: The dog bounding toward her and a muffled gasp of surprise from the drunk man. When the dog leaped to clear the hedge, she fired the second dart, hitting the animal in his chest. He collapsed midair, crashing in a furry heap on top of the shrub, inches from her thighs.

Without missing a beat, Adams lunged over the hedge, driving the pistol's barrel into the drunk's throat. He gagged and choked as he staggered backward, flailing his arms. Planting her left foot, Adams launched a roundhouse kick with her right that caught him under his chin, snapping his head back. He flew off his feet before landing unconscious, faceup in front of the SUVs, arms extended as if he had been crucified.

"Mayday," she said into her mike while running toward the barn. "Let's do this quickly."

She grabbed the rope and, with Bolan's assistance from above, scaled the wall to the loft.

"My watch is picking up trace radiation," Bolan said, directing the beam from his powerful penlight to the area below. From their position, they could see a work area with two protective suits hanging from hooks on the wall. There was no one inside the barn.

"I'm going down. Get outside and stand guard," Bolan said.

Adams nodded and slid back down the thin cord, hitting the ground on the run. The privet hedge was planted on a small berm of earth that Adams thought would afford a certain level of small-arms cover. She sprinted behind the shrubs, diving to a spot close to where the guard dog lay unconscious.

Reaching up to pull the dog out of sight, she had her hand on his collar when a man came out of the farmhouse onto the porch and yelled, "Hey!" in her direction.

He was quickly joined by three others who burst through the door with guns at the ready. Seconds after Adams hugged the earth for all she was worth, they opened fire, hosing the area with 9 mm rounds. The slugs ripped the dog's body to shreds, showering Adams with a torrent of bloody fur. Staying low, she pulled her SIG-Sauer from her hip holster as she heard the deep-throated rapid fire of a new weapon.

The Executioner charged around the corner of the barn, his face illuminated by the flashes spitting from his submachine gun as it threw a wall of lead before him. One of the gunmen was flung straight back by Bolan's first volley, his weapon firing into the air as he crashed lifeless through the porch railing. The two remaining men scrambled for cover while their unarmed companion dashed into the house a millisecond before the remaining wooden railings on the porch exploded into thousands of splinters as Bolan exhausted his first 50-round magazine and reached for another.

One of the gunmen jumped to his feet and dashed forward, his gun chattering on full-auto.

Bolan hit the dirt and rolled behind the cover of an outcropping of rock while ramming a new magazine into the Spectre's ammo port. Lethal rounds chewed up clods of earth all around him, bullets buzzing through the air above his head.

From her prone position behind the hedges, Adams fired her SIG-Sauer, the weapon's husky roar sounding thrice within two seconds as she hit the man charging Bolan first in his hip, then under his arm and, finally, below his ear, the last round blowing half his skull away in a crimson cloud of bone chips and brain tissue. The man's momentum carried him three steps forward before he crashed to the ground.

From a well-covered position behind a corner of the porch, the remaining gunman fired in Bolan's direction, filling the night with the repeating stutter of autofire. A cascade of bullets struck the rocks protecting Bolan, sending jagged chips on oblique flight patterns into the dark sky.

With Bolan returning fire in short bursts, Adams seized the opportunity to maneuver to her right, where the angle of engagement would be more favorable. Firing as she ran, she hit the gunman in his right shoulder, spinning him for an exposed shot to the neck. Her next bullet tore through his carotid artery, ending his life.

The farmhouse door flew open and the man who had sounded the alarm rushed out, a sawed-off Remington shotgun held waist high. He hesitated for an instant, as if deciding which target to engage, but, before his brain compiled the answer, he was hammered back through the door with a long staccato burst of lead.

The night was suddenly silent.

"Let's go," Bolan said as he raced past. Adams jumped to her feet and ran after him. They sprinted full out for about three minutes, almost stepping on the first dog and guard they had encountered.

The revving of an engine sounded behind them seconds before the beam of a spotlight threw their shadows onto a stone wall a few yards to the front. Their pursuers abruptly opened fire and the heart-stopping din of automatic weapons once again filled the night.

With rounds buzzing like angry hornets all around them, Bolan and Adams dived over the wall.

As she cleared the rocks, Adams felt a flash of heat on her scalp, followed by the stink of scorched hair when she hit the ground beyond.

"Take this," Bolan said, passing her the submachine gun while he pulled the MK-23 from his shoulder holster.

She peeked over the wall and cut loose with a long volley of 9 mm rounds that ricocheted with sparks and whines upon impacting the approaching vehicle.

"Armor plated," she said breathlessly as she ducked down.

Bolan ejected the magazine loaded into his weapon and replaced it with one he pulled from his shirt pocket. Scuttling to his left to get out of the spotlight trained on their position, he rose to one knee and fired two quick shots.

The SUV exploded in an eyeball-searing inferno. The vehicle was lifted off the ground, coming to rest upside down in a blazing heap of twisted metal.

Bolan rose to his full height and fired the remaining Orvilles at the SUVs parked in the driveway. They exploded as spectacularly as the first, spewing burning debris onto the farmhouse, which quickly became engulfed in flames as Bolan and Adams resumed their flight to the trees.

"No strontium," Bolan said as they stepped into the woods

and began the exaggerated high-stepping stride they had used on the way in.

"Damn! It was there, though?"

"Yeah. There were still traces, and you saw the moon suits. I grabbed a bunch of paperwork."

Adams was wheezing, each breath labored.

"Are you okay?"

"I got clipped. Just a scalp wound."

She started to say something else when her foot landed on a hard plate, a loud metallic click sounded, and she and Bolan froze dead in their tracks. "Son of a bitch!"

While Adams remained motionless, Bolan pushed away the branches and brush on the right side of the path. Finding nothing, he moved across the trail to the other side.

"Here it is," he said, pointing to a plastic box with wires running into the ground. "It looks like buckshot." Bolan leaned close to the booby trap. "These are the ends of shotgun shells."

He unhooked his web belt, lay his weapons on the ground and walked about ten yards down the path before turning around.

"Flying tackle," he said. "Just go with the flow and make sure you're looking away."

Adams nodded.

"I'll have to hit you hard for us to clear."

"Do it," she said.

Bolan took a deep breath and sprinted as fast as he could toward Adams. When he was a few feet away, he launched himself horizontally through the air, crashing his shoulder into her rib cage while he turned his body to expose his side and back to the blast, shielding her as best he could.

The shotgun shells detonated the instant her weight left the pressure plate, spraying Bolan with buckshot all the way from his shoulder to below his buttocks. His clothes shredded and the raw skin underneath looked like he had spilled a speeding motorcycle onto a road strewed with pebbles. It was as painful as being singed with a blowtorch. His leg immediately began to bleed badly.

Bolan landed hard on top of Adams, compressing her ribs and forcing the wind from her lungs. Unable to breathe, she squirmed out from under him, struggling to suck in air. Bolan could tell she was teetering on the brink of unconsciousness as she pulled herself onto her hands and knees, letting her head droop forward while she swayed from side to side until her forehead rested on the ground. Only then did her lungs slowly fill with short gasps of air that Bolan knew were burning as if molten lead was being poured down her throat.

"You okay?" she croaked.

He grunted and edged forward with a crawling motion that slowly evolved into an elbows and knees position before he was able to will himself upright. Staggering forward, his left side soaked with blood, he bent to retrieve his web belt and weapon.

"Close," he muttered.

Adams didn't know if he meant that the car was close by or that they had just escaped a close call—but it was, and they had. She forced herself to her feet, realizing from the sudden pain that the back of her left thigh had been grazed with buckshot. She reached her hand down to feel the area and, although it came away bloody, she knew she was not losing a serious amount.

When they reached the car, Adams said, "I'm good to drive."

Bolan lay across the backseat and began to pick lead pellets out of his flesh, which he dropped, bloody and sticky, onto the Volvo's rear floor mats.

THROUGH THE PULSATING JETS of hot water cascading over his head, Bolan could hear Adams moving outside the shower curtain as she lit the candles throughout the bathroom. The flowery fragrances released by the burning wax quickly infused the steamy air with an ambiance reminiscent of spas in the South Pacific.

Adams switched off the lights, and the shower was enveloped with a soft flickering light that sent shadows dancing like pixies across the tile walls.

Except for the nagging attention demanded by his throbbing shoulder and side, Bolan's mind was as close to shutting down as it ever got, although the war-tested soldier was no stranger to this semiconscious state when his body began the recovery process. Behind his slitted eyes, Bolan's warrior mind was taking inventory of his heart rate and breathing; his blood loss and muscle functions. This time, the wounds were superficial. He'd be sore for a few days, but he had been through worse.

Adams parted the curtain and stepped in at the foot of the tub. Bolan peered over his shoulder, finding the bathroom's subdued light soothing to his tired eyeballs. He inhaled deeply, and the fragrant steam radiated waves of relaxation throughout his lungs.

Adams was holding a tube of antibacterial ointment from which she squeezed a healthy dollop into the palm of her right hand. She was wearing a cotton sports bra that flattened the swell of her firm breasts and high-cut white silk panties. As she took a step forward into the water, she winced as the hot needles hit the outside of her thigh where she sported a smaller version of the buckshot raspberry that covered Bolan's entire side from shoulder to buttocks.

"Let me treat this," she said, reaching out to smear the ointment onto Bolan's wound. "I'm not coming on to you."

He nodded, too exhausted to be thinking carnal thoughts, regardless of his proximity to the woman's body. He turned his shoulder to her, and she applied the balm, rubbing it into his wound with firm, sure strokes.

The stream from the showerhead was ricocheting off Bolan's wide back, soaking Adams from head to foot. "Turn," she said.

She squeezed more ointment onto her hand and rubbed it into the raw tissue under Bolan's arm, careful not to break the wet scabs that were forming. Holding her hands under the water, she washed off the excess before moving back to the foot of the tub.

"Out," she said not unkindly. "My turn."

Bolan nodded and pulled the curtain aside. "Thanks," he said, stepping out of the tub.

He grabbed a towel from the rack on the wall and dried himself with a few quick strokes before shuffling into the bedroom. From his travel bag he retrieved a clean set of shorts, which he pulled on before getting into the king-sized bed that was positioned to afford its occupants a distant view of mountains. Within minutes he was dead to the world, not stirring in the slightest when Adams slid onto the far side of the mattress where she fell asleep almost as quickly as he had.

Bolan was the last to arrive, and Brognola watched him move to the open seat at the conference table.

"Are you hurt?"

"Just a little stiff."

Brognola glanced across at Katey, who wore a small bandage on the top of her head where she parted her hair. "Your soft probe ended up being not so soft," he said.

"They moved the strontium before we got there," Bolan stated flatly.

"Which is where we can start," Aaron Kurtzman said from his place at the head of the table.

He pointed a remote at the wall and pushed a button that simultaneously dimmed the overhead lights while causing a flat-screen wall monitor to appear. On the screen, a real-time map of the Atlantic Ocean was displayed, with tens of thousands of data points shown in various colors.

"Let's hear from Akira," Kurtzman said.

"Ocean traffic," Tokaido said. "We're using a process of elimination. The strontium went to Ireland to be processed into a dirty bomb. Let's assume that's already happened. Step two, get the bomb to its target, presumably the United States. With today's security, you can't get it here on an airplane. Therefore, it will come into Mexico, Canada or directly into the States via ship. These data points—" he motioned to the screen "—are vessels. Our job now is to find the right one."

"How do you know we haven't missed it?" Brognola asked. "It could already be at its destination."

"I don't think so," Tokaido said. "The strontium was stolen in Georgia less than two weeks ago. Some of these data points are real-time. Also on this display are overlays of everything that left Ireland in the past week. For ships already at their destination we're employing regression analysis. We'll eventually find the most probable ship."

"Eventually," Brognola said, "may not be soon enough."

"Understood. We're going as fast as we can."

"Who owned the farm we hit?" Bolan asked.

"Dead end," Carmen Delahunt answered. "We've already chased that to ground. Owned for ten years by a name that's untraceable. Doesn't exist. No link to either the North or South."

"How about the paperwork I took?"

"Nothing there to help us locate the strontium. No shipping invoices or anything like that, but there were orders for supplies. It looks like Cypher is assembling a small army. Thirty, forty soldiers maybe."

"A bit fewer after the night before last," Adams said, looking across the table at Bolan.

Brognola frowned and asked, "How dangerous is the strontium? What's the worst case that we're facing here?"

"Not nuclear," Tokaido said. "Dirty bombs are referred to as weapons of mass disruption. The death and destruction caused by a dirty bomb going off is no greater than that of a conventional explosion. The disruption occurs because the area becomes contaminated, people have to be evacuated and, before the site can be used again, EPA personnel have to clean the place up."

"How bad is that?"

Tokaido shrugged. "In rural settings, not bad at all. Scrape away a few feet of the earth, bury it at sea, and it degrades over time with insignificant ecological impact. In a city it's much worse because concrete and granite absorb and retain radiation. Buildings have to be demolished and pulverized before they're disposed of. An area with granite buildings might take years to be useable again."

"A city, then, with a population that would be injured in the initial blast and then be disrupted for who knows how long with a demolition and reconstruction, appears to be the ideal target for a dirty bomb," Wethers said in summary.

"Exactly. And then there's the psychological impact. Radiation is scary no matter what your government is telling you," Tokaido added.

There were a few moments of silence before Brognola changed the subject by asking, "Where are we on validating the evidence?"

"Hunt and I ran a series of scenarios," Kurtzman answered, "and determined that a change in the status quo produces no discernable gain for anyone outside of Ireland. Therefore, we conclude that it's either the North, as the communiqué states—or it's the South trying to frame the North.

"If the United States gives in to the demands and forces a settlement, the North wins. They get undisputed sovereignty, the IRA disarms and the decades-old struggle ends. If, however, an attack does occur and the United States strikes back at whom they believe to be the terrorists, the South wins by getting the U.S. to wipe out their enemies, forcing the Brits to abolish the government that harbored the terrorists and reunite Ireland under home rule," Wethers stated.

"Unfortunately, both sides present a viable case. We need a stronger tie, one way or the other," Kurtzman added.

"Not good," Brognola said. "We need some hard evidence so we can nail this onto someone, once and for all. Time's running out."

Gregory McKenna stared at the string of numbers sequencing real-time on his computer monitor. The succession of digits held his full attention because he received messages formatted this way so rarely, and the few times when he did, it meant only one thing.

The figures scrolling across his screen had been traveling for almost a day through cyberspace, pausing for microseconds in hundreds of virtual mailboxes, encrypted and re-encrypted at each stop before being forwarded to the next station. The process would continue for another few hours, leaving in its wake tens of thousands of numerical sequences. All but one were meaningless.

McKenna applied his cipher and waited for it to reveal the transmission's message.

It was three lines of text, the first requesting a meeting the next morning at coordinates he immediately identified as Trafalgar Square. The second line was the phrase, "Countless squab roost this morning." The third, "They find safety in numbers."

How he would recognize his contact was not mentioned.

Contrary to what most members of the Irish underground believed, McKenna was neither an agent of the British government nor a member of the Orange Order. He occasionally received confirmation of terrorist activities through secure military conduits such as the one where this message was presumably originating. Less often, when the judicial system failed and vengeance was justified, he took action. He received orders from no man, reported to none. In the eight years since his family's death, McKenna had killed fourteen men operating from three separate IRA cells linked to railway bombings. Never before had a face-to-face meeting been requested.

He punched a series of keys, initiating a subroutine in the encryption program. His CPU hummed for a few seconds before telling him the transmission came from a military source and held a blue security code. Blue undoubtedly meant the sender had access to a Cray Supercomputer—the only machines with enough number-crunching power to generate the volume of sequences required to reach this level of encryption. It also meant the subject matter was considered vital to his country's national security.

McKenna rubbed his temples while staring at the message. He didn't like the idea of a meeting. There were few people who knew of him to begin with. The tabloids occasionally speculated about his existence, but, lacking concrete evidence, their tales of an avenging vigilante driven by personal tragedy took on the semblance of a legend. Most people, he was sure, dismissed them as such. That was how he wanted it—how his wife and two daughters, killed eight years previously by an IRA pipe bomb, would have wanted it.

McKenna looked at his watch, calculated there were eight hours until the requested meeting. The square was safe at any time of the day or night. At seven in the morning, it would be jammed with commuters, tourists and various groups of locals beginning their day.

Something big was in the works. The message appeared

to be authentic, the encryption valid. It was almost certainly coming from his occasional military sources, whoever they were. And, since they were as blind to his identity as he was to theirs, he would be able to control the action. If things didn't feel right, he wouldn't initiate contact.

McKenna leaned over his keyboard and began typing an e-mail. If, within the next week he did not cancel delivery, it would automatically be sent to Inspector Tom Wynsten, his friend at Scotland Yard.

Trafalgar Square, he told himself before going to bed, would be safe.

THE MORNING WAS WARM and sunny, holding the promise of a glorious day. A troop of schoolchildren skipped across Trafalgar Square under the watchful eyes of two nuns dressed in the Dominican Order's abbreviated habits. Their drab brown-and-white garb set them apart from the brilliant maroon-and-blue uniforms of their wards, evoking an image of soldiers assigned to guard a stash of priceless gems.

Scurrying commuters crossed paths with tourists heading into the subway, contributing, for a few moments, to the kaleidoscopic patterns of humanity that ebbed and swelled in phase with London's train schedules. Red double-decker buses took on their passengers from stops around the square, departing for points throughout the city in a routine analogous to Trafalgar himself, who had repeatedly set out for distant points on the globe.

A small group of women wearing black burkas with matching chadors hung together like a flock, scattering grain as they made their way slowly across the wide concrete apron. Trafalgar Square's pigeons congregated about their feet.

A British officer strode past the women as if he were passing in review, his shadow as ramrod straight as the one cast by Nelson's Column. The man held a blue folder under his arm. He took a seat on a bench close to the fountains and idly watched the people feeding the birds.

After a few minutes, one of the burka-clad women strolled close, leading a parade of softly cooing pigeons.

"Countless squab roost this morning," a deep voice said.

The phrase brought a slight smile to the officer's face. He noticed one of McKenna's hands remained hidden within the folds of the burka and knew with certainty that a gun was pointed at his heart.

"They find safety in numbers," he replied without removing his gaze from the tourists. "I've been instructed to inform you of two things. First, the IRA is planning a series of terrorist attacks against grade schools. Second, you also are a target."

"When?"

"Soon is all we know. We believe the attack on you is imminent. A certain deputy minister has asked that you come with me. He holds information he can release only to you. In person."

McKenna paused and scattered the last of his grain onto the ground.

"And if I say no to the meeting?"

"We will ask that you reconsider. If there is a better time and a better place, we will accommodate you. But, please understand, time runs short. Innocent lives are at stake."

Through his tentlike chador, McKenna studied the officer. The previous night's message, he had decided, was authentic. There was no way an outsider could gain access to a Cray Supercomputer in order to break the military's encryption. Previous messages had come in the same manner through the Defense Ministry, and the people who'd sent this officer knew his blue folder would be recognized as a reference to the previous night's security code. Finally, the man's verbal contact had been correct.

Still, he didn't like meetings.

As if he could read McKenna's mind, the officer repeated, "The lives of innocent children are at stake."

The silence hung heavy between them.

"I have a white Volvo parked across from the South Africa House on Duncannon," the officer said. "I'll go there now and wait for ten minutes."

He stood, straightened his cap and, without another glance at McKenna, strode away.

THEY HAD BEEN RIDING in silence for close to half an hour when Lieutenant Colonel William Palmer, the associate dean of electronics at Sandhurst Academy, suddenly asked, "Are you going to keep that thing pointed at me the whole way?"

"How much longer?" McKenna asked in return.

He still wore the burka and chador. The weapon Palmer referred to had not been displayed. But neither had McKenna's right hand.

"We're almost there."

McKenna knew exactly where they were. Years ago, before the attack that took his family, he had belonged to a hunting club that came to these woods for quail and wild boar. There were numerous cabins scattered throughout, ideal settings for a deputy minister to meet with someone who did not exist.

Palmer slowed and turned off the highway onto a dirt road leading through thick brush that quickly morphed into dense trees. After another ten minutes, they arrived at a small cabin. He stopped the car, switched off the ignition and reached for the door handle.

"Wait," McKenna said, turning slightly to better accommodate the pistol he held beneath his burka.

Palmer froze.

"Where's the deputy's auto?"

"He said he'd hike in from a spot not too distant. Out for a hunt, in the event he's seen. I should tell you not to be alarmed that he most certainly will be carrying a shotgun." He shifted his gaze to the cabin. "I imagine he's inside, although, I see no sign of him."

"Very well," McKenna said. "Let's get out together and walk to the cabin. I would like you to stay in front of me."

Palmer nodded and opened his door. As he stepped out, he slid the Silver Arrow throwing knife secured to the underside of his forearm from its catch.

McKenna's face was clearly visible through the flimsy chador. At such close range, his eye was an easy target for a man who had once been his university's dart champion.

Palmer's arm moved in a blur, and McKenna went down without a sound, the thin handle of the throwing knife protruding from his right eye socket.

Palmer lunged behind the front fender of the Volvo where he crouched and began counting seconds. The brain was a funny thing. He knew of men who had taken a bullet through the head, yet managed to live for up to half a minute—plenty of time to squeeze off an avenging round.

When a full minute had passed, he stood upright and stretched his neck to study the body. Confident that McKenna was, indeed, dead, he walked briskly to the rear of the Volvo, opened the trunk and removed a wooden case, a small sack of plaster of Paris and a jug of water.

Less than an hour later his work was done, and the body of Gregory McKenna—the late great avenger of senseless civilian bombings—lay in a shallow grave on the grounds of a semiprivate hunting reserve.

Despite being narrow and pocked with potholes, the street—and most others like it in the area—serviced more than five hundred trucks daily, hauling goods from the receiving docks to warehouses throughout New Jersey. Lighting at night in this section was poor, shadows were rich and textured, and Mack Bolan felt completely at home in the hostile environment.

He was dressed in black from head to toe, with a longshoreman's wool knit cap covering his hair. Beneath his loose-fitting windbreaker, he wore two shoulder holsters, one holding his trusty .44-caliber Desert Eagle, the other his Beretta 93-R. On his web belt he carried a pouch containing, among other things, an electronic device roughly the size and shape of two decks of playing cards that Tokaido had assembled to help him skirt the security cameras he would encounter at his destination.

The import company determined as the most likely recipient of the strontium shipment from Ireland was about a quarter of a mile away at the end of the street. Its harbor side was constructed over the water to accommodate an industrial dock capable of unloading sea containers directly from ocean-going vessels.

While most of the commerce passing through this town was legitimate, a healthy portion was not.

Noise from a sidewalk bar reached Bolan's ears when he was still half a block away. He could tell from the raucous sounds that it was the type of establishment found in dock areas around the world, offering men who had been at sea a place to drink and fight. Above the scratchy country music spilling into the street, Bolan could hear men's voices raised in anger as alcohol and drugs lubricated their slide into violence. An entwined group of four men came tumbling out the open door, swearing loudly as they pummeled one another to the ground, landing in a rolling tangle of arms and legs among the filthy layer of cigarette butts and decomposing trash that lined the gutter. Bolan stepped into the middle of the street to go around them, his combat boots treading silently as he passed.

The import company was fronted by a huge parking lot filled with row upon row of sea containers awaiting disposition. Not wanting to be in the layover business, the owners charged a hefty fee for every hour of storage, with the result that most of these containers would be gone within days. The entire property was enclosed by a chain-link fence topped with concertino barbed wire, giving the compound the aura of a combat perimeter.

As Bolan walked past, he took note of the distant warehouse with security cameras mounted above doors and windows protected by heavy metal grates streaked with rust. Vestiges of the hellfire trail buried deep in his subconscious triggered suppressed memories of barb-wired compounds half a world away, bringing him to full alert.

He continued more than two blocks beyond the edge of the parking lot, giving his mind time to process the facts of his quick recon before he turned and started his approach.

A gang of teenage hoodlums sauntered into the middle of the street from an alley ahead, their arrogance indicative of what they believed was their superior strength. They formed themselves into a line, the two at the ends holding stubby aluminum bats that they repeatedly tapped into their open palms while staring with icy eyes at Bolan.

He walked straight toward the youth in the center, counting the others as he approached. There were seven, a number he was comfortable taking on, but he hoped to avoid a confrontation that would only delay his mission. At about ten feet away, Bolan stopped.

"My business is not your business," he said calmly. "Let me pass."

"Whatcha got in that Army belt, G.I. Joe?" the youth in the middle said, sneering with the disdain of a bully who always got his way.

"Nothing for you."

"We'll see," he said, while taking a few steps forward and reaching for Bolan's jacket.

Bolan shot his left arm forward, driving two stiff fingers into the youth's armpit. The teen froze for a second, as if an electric current were passing through his body, before he howled in pain and dropped to the sidewalk, his right arm dangling lifelessly. Furiously kicking his legs, he scuttled backward the way an injured hermit crab would retreat.

"Fucker!" he yelled. "Get him!"

The others rushed forward in a disorganized assault, the ones in the center reaching Bolan seconds before the thugs on the ends, giving him the opportunity to engage them individually. He stepped forward, jabbing with both hands, his left knuckles smashing the nose of his first assailant, sending him to the ground spurting blood like water from an open fire hydrant. A nanosecond later, he jabbed the windpipe of the one charging him on the right. The teenager staggered back a step, making choking sounds as he went straight down. A low roundhouse kick launched at the knee of one of the two carrying bats landed dead on target, with Bolan's steel-toed boot knocking the patella to the side with such force that he could hear the tendons pop as they tore free. The youth dropped the bat and crumpled into the street, whimpering and clutching his destroyed knee.

Without breaking his momentum from the kick, Bolan surged forward, striking one of thc punks with an exploding elbow to the chin that snapped the kid's head back, rendering him unconscious as he left his feet.

Spinning, Bolan turned to face the remaining two. They were less than six feet apart when the one without the bat reached into his back pocket, his hand coming forward with an imitation pearl-handled stiletto. With a dismissive scowl, Bolan drew his Desert Eagle.

The two stared in disbelief at the massive pistol for a long second before dropping their weapons.

"Pick up your wounded and get out of here," Bolan gritted through his teeth.

Clutching his arm tight against his ribs, the leader staggered to his feet, his eyes flashing the fury of a rabid dog. He barked a few orders, and the uninjured teenagers began to help their comrades reach the alley they had come from.

Bolan backed away, keeping his Desert Eagle trained in their direction lest they attempt a foolish last strike. Less than a minute after their departure, he heard the revving of a car engine followed by the scream of tires peeling out.

If they come back, he thought, they'll have guns.

Pushing away the thought that he might end up killing them all, he turned in body and mind toward his objective, pausing for a moment to kick the discarded aluminum bat at his feet and send it rolling with a hollow metallic sound into the gutter.

The back corner of the chain-link fence on the parking lot's harbor side was shrouded in angular shadows from the boxcar-sized shipping units, making it the ideal spot for entry into the storage yard. Using a pair of wire clippers, Bolan snipped a cutout he could slide through and, once inside, ran for the closest sea container.

Pressed against the corrugated iron, he waited for the sound of an alarm. When he was convinced none was forthcoming, he stepped forward, flitting as silently as a shadow between the tall containers that stood in straight rows like caskets on a military runway awaiting their final trip home.

As he came close to the building, Bolan saw there was a spotlight and motion detector halfway up the wall facing him. Dropping to one knee, he drew the Beretta from his shoulder holster while, with his other hand, he fished the pistol's sound suppressor from his pouch. After attaching the suppressor to the barrel, he stabilized himself by leaning into the side of the sea container next to him. He took careful aim and squeezed off a single round. The light exploded with a soft pop, sending a cascade of shards onto the asphalt. Pieces of glass hitting the pavement sounded loud against the night, and Bolan remained motionless, waiting for a reaction. After a minute had passed, he resumed his approach.

On the long side of the building facing the water, there was a huge dock with two industrial cranes capable of picking loaded sea containers off arriving ships and depositing them onto waiting flatbeds to be delivered or stored in the yard. As he moved silently onto the dock and took up position behind a piling painted black and sticky with a thick coat of creosote, he noticed that one of the cranes was angled toward the building, its tip extending out over the roof.

Bolan slipped his night-vision goggles over his eyes, switched them to infrared mode. He instantly picked out the closed-circuit camera mounted under the dock awning. He pulled the electronic assembly from his pouch, removed a thin strip of protective wrap from the adhesive side of the housing and pressed the device onto the piling. Peering through the peep sight built into the top of the case, he used two thumbwheels controlling pitch and cant to aim the assembly's lens at the camera. Once he was satisfied that the module was properly aimed, he pushed the power button on the back of the housing, and a tiny LED glowed red for a few seconds, then green, indicating that a feedback loop had been established and all was operational.

Thus shielded from the surveillance camera by electronic cover, Bolan stood to his full height and walked quickly to the crane overhanging the roof. He checked his holsters as he went, making sure his weapons were secure. When he reached the crane, he pulled himself onto the boom. Using a hand-over-hand motion, he ascended skyward as deftly as a fireman making a rescue. Reaching a spot above the roof, he lowered himself to hang by his arms, damping his sway by flexing his biceps. When he had halted his motion, he dropped silently onto the sea-weathered shingles.

At the peak of the roofline were three large air vents, protected from the elements by metal panels comprised of louvered slats. Bolan scampered up the slope to the vents. With the edge of his wire clippers, he pried loose one of the panels that had patches of rust around its edges. Putting his shoulder into the frame, he bent the thin metal outward, opening a space big enough for him to squeeze through.

As Bolan had feared, there was nothing for him to stand on directly below the air vents. He could hang by his arms, but, even with his height, there was a span of another six feet before he'd reach the heavy four-by-eight joists that supported the roof. From the joists, there was an additional drop of about ten feet onto one of the wooden crates that filled the wide-open second floor.

A second before he was ready to slide through the open air vent, footsteps sounded below. He promptly drew back, his hand reaching instinctively for the Desert Eagle.

A man with a submachine gun slung across his chest walked below him, quickly progressing to a point where his view of the air vents became obscured by the tall wooden crates. He paused for a few seconds when he reached the end of the row, then turned and walked on. His footsteps faded into silence.

Bolan eased himself through the open air vent, dropping feetfirst to the joist below. The wooden beam vibrated and swayed under his weight, but he held his balance until he was able to make a controlled hop to the top of the wooden crate under him. From there, he lowered himself to the floor.

With the guard's submachine gun at the forefront of his mind, he set off in the other direction to find a stairway leading down to the first floor. As he went, he drew his Beretta.

The stairway to the ground floor was at the far end of the building and, at the foot of it, was the manager's office with its door half open. Through the open space, Bolan could see two men snorting cocaine off the top of the desk.

Remaining in the shadows of the stairwell, he sneaked toward the door. When he reached the bottom of the stairs, he rushed into the office, pulling the door closed behind him.

"Hands up," he said to the astonished trio, the third of whom was behind the desk and had not been visible from the stairs.

They turned confused faces toward the new arrival.

"I said hands up," Bolan repeated with an edge to his voice.

The man behind the desk made a frantic grab under the leg well, but before he had a chance to show Bolan what he was reaching for, the Beretta coughed once. The man's head jerked back as a hole the size of a dime appeared in the middle of his forehead and the wall behind was splashed with brain matter. Eyes wide and unseeing, he fell forward onto the desktop, blood from his head wound seeping toward the little mound of white powder sitting on a piece of glass.

The remaining two thrust their hands over their heads, their glassy eyes displaying absolute terror.

"Please, please, wc…we didn't tell no one," one of them gasped.

"Tell no one, what?" Bolan asked.

"About the shipment."

"The shipment from Ireland?"

They both nodded.

"Get against that wall," Bolan said, motioning with the pistol so he could move to a spot away from the door.

They did as they were told, clearly confused and dismayed at the turn of events.

"Tell me about the shipment," Bolan said.

They hesitated, perhaps realizing through their stupor that Bolan was one of the people they weren't supposed to tell.

"Day before yesterday. We was going to see what was inside, but it had them radiation stickers and we decided not to. Crazy motherfuckers came to pick it up," one of the men blurted out.

"Crazy, how?"

"Nervous. Jitterylike. We was glad to get rid of them."

"Where did they go?"

"Don't know."

Bolan reached forward, positioning the Beretta inches from the man's nose.

"Last chance. Where did they go?"

The man was hyperventilating, his runny red eyes blinking against a stream of sweat that poured in a torrent down his forehead.

"They was, they—" he swallowed hard, as if the words were caught in his throat "—was Lucino's men. One of them said something about Lucino's warehouse in Queens. Maybe that's where they was going."

"Both of you. Down on the floor. Hands behind you."

Before they had a chance to obey Bolan's command, he heard the unmistakable sound of a pump-action shotgun being cocked outside the office door. He threw himself toward the far corner of the room, landing behind a metal file cabinet a split second before the flimsy door exploded in a hurricane of lead pellets and wood splinters. Immediately following the shotgun blast, the eardrum-popping stutter of 5.56 mm automatic gunfire erupted, slicing the two men Bolan had been interrogating. Under the steady stream of lethal slugs pouring through the door, their lifeless bodies jerked and danced, spitting blood and guts in every direction.

The submachine gun abruptly stopped firing. Knowing that the gunman was reloading, Bolan sprang from behind the file cabinet and rushed forward, his Desert Eagle roaring death from his left hand while the Beretta spit 9 mm rounds from his right.

The heavy bullets from the Desert Eagle hammered the man with the sawed-off shotgun, opening a trio of fist-sized holes in his chest. The guard with the submachine gun dived out of Bolan's line of fire, dropping the magazine he was attempting to load into his Colt.

Bolan launched himself through the open space in a horizontal dive. As he passed the man who was fumbling in panic with another magazine, the Executioner fired both weapons. The angry retort of his Desert Eagle reverberated throughout the warehouse as the guard's face was blown with the acceleration of an express locomotive through the back of his head. The Beretta's 9 mm rounds also found their mark, gratuitously slamming the dead body against a wooden crate that suddenly looked as if it had been painted red by a very sloppy employee.

Bolan hit the ground and continued to roll, in case these two were not alone. He found cover behind a wooden crate with stenciled markings for shipment to Bermuda and peered out from behind. After a minute of his breathing being the only sound he could hear above the residual ringing in his ears, he knew there were no other combatants in the building.

He holstered his weapons and walked to the door exiting onto the dock. On the way back to his point of entry in the chain-link fence, he stopped to retrieve the electronic module from the top of the piling.

Lucino, he thought.

Of course one of the New Jersey Families would be involved in everything that passed illegally across these docks.

Bolan had gone up against the Mob many times and, while others may have hesitated at the prospect of confronting organized crime, Bolan's only emotion was an odd twinge of nostalgia.

At this point, those who stood in the Executioner's way would pay the price.

"Lucino is bad news," Brognola said, sliding a heavy manila folder across the conference table to Bolan. "Last fall, the FBI lost six agents trying to infiltrate that warehouse. Not to mention what those animals did to Judge Champlain's family."

Bolan opened the file and began reading while members of Kurtzman's cybernetics team filtered into the room.

Brognola continued to talk, paraphrasing the documents Bolan was scanning. "Judge Champlain issued a warrant to search Lucino's warehouses last February when the FBI finally obtained sufficient evidence to establish probable cause. Within a week, one of his daughters was shot in the back of the head, execution style. And that wasn't all they did to her. It was a brutal message.

"The judge and his family were devastated, but they thought if they gave in, the daughter's death would be in vain. Instead, Mrs. Champlain and the other three kids moved into a safehouse with 24/7 protection.

"Before the warrant was even executed, security at the safehouse was breached. Two guards, Mrs. Champlain and one of the sons were shot. The judge withdrew the warrant and retired to South Dakota, taking his two remaining children with him."

"The safehouse was federal?" Bolan asked.

Brognola nodded. "U.S. Marshals."

In response to Bolan's raised eyebrows, the big Fed reached forward and pulled a black-and-white photo from the file. In the picture, a clean-cut man in his late thirties or early forties was getting into a black Ferrari. He was dressed in tennis whites and was staring back at the camera with cold hard eyes, his mouth drawn into the type of smirk that conveyed distain for everyone and everything.

"Marcus Arnold, Lucino's Family lawyer. He's as dirty as they come. Apparently, Feds say he used his contacts in the attorney general's office to find the safehouse. Nothing is traceable—no ties to the Family."

Bolan flipped through the remaining documents in the folder, coming back and pausing for a long moment to stare at the lawyer's photo.

"We've made some progress," Kurtzman said from the end of the table, bringing the meeting to order.

"I hope so," Brognola retorted. "There's only one week left in July. The communiqué gave the United States until the end of the month to endorse Northern Ireland's sovereignty. We're almost out of time."

"I'm aware of the deadline," Kurtzman answered. He turned toward Wethers, said, "Tell us about McKenna."

"As you all know," Wethers began, his voice immediately taking on the tone of a lecturing professor, "McKenna is rumored to be the vigilante responsible for a score of IRA murders. No one knows his identity, but fingerprints that Scotland Yard believes are his have been recovered from a number of crime scenes. There are no matches in any of the databases."

"It's not unusual for someone to go through life without ever being fingerprinted. McKenna was obviously never in the service, he never held a security clearance and he's never been arrested," Kurtzman said.

"Two days ago, British authorities raided a depot in Londonderry. They contacted Ed Fontes because among other things, they found this." Wethers held up a compact disc. "Before we play it, you should know that the fingerprints Scotland Yard thinks are McKenna's were on the CD as well as on many other items in the depot."

Wethers inserted the CD into a player and pressed the play button.

The silence in the room was filled with a soft hissing for a few moments before a voice came over the speaker:

"American cousins, you grieve today for one of your leaders. Look beyond your hearts to what he was: An emissary of Rome, determined to help his people in their lawless revolution against the Crown. This is not America's war. The conflict in Ireland will end when lawless Catholics disarm and recognize the legitimacy of the loyalists. Grieve not, cousins, but join us in our strength on this historical holiday. Join with us to stop the Catholic conspiracy. Morta La Papa!"

There was a quiet click followed by the soft hiss. Wethers turned off the player and said, "They expect the United States to ignore their demands. This CD was intended to be released after their attack."

"McKenna gives us a strong tie to the North," Brognola said.

"Strong enough for a preemptive strike against the Orange Order?" Kurtzman asked.

Brognola shook his head slowly. "That's not our decision."

"Who's the leader they plan on killing and what's the historical holiday?" Tokaido asked. "Death to the Pope?"

Wethers nodded while consulting a yellow legal pad. The top sheet was covered with notes handwritten in blue ink.

"Katey Adams said her editor friend—" he paused to look at the notes "—Bryan McGuinness, told her there's an assassination list with his, Moore's, Foley's and the Pope's names. This message refers to a man. The leader they're coming after must be Daniel Foley.

"The secretary is visiting West Point on August 17, which happens to be the start of Marching Season when Protestants parade through Catholic neighborhoods celebrating a seventeenth-century victory by a group of Apprentice boys over the Catholic army of King James."

"The historical holiday," Delahunt said. "Let's not forget that the communiqué was sent by a group calling themselves the Apprentices."

"Can you all see the manipulation?" Bolan asked, "And how Katey's drugging fits in?"

The others turned to him, and he explained.

"Katey is the officer in charge of Foley's trip to West Point. She's the only one who knows his schedules, the timetables and the security plan. By killing those three agents, Cypher finessed the CIA into sending their only expert—Katey Adams—back to Ireland. He knew she was in charge of planning cabinet trips and that she would have information he could use to plan an attack."

Bolan paused for a second, frowning. "The nurse in the emergency room is a link. I'm sure she was working with them."

"I'll have someone pick her up," Brognola broke in. "Your mission, Striker, is to find the strontium, which, most likely, has already been processed into a dirty bomb. If August 17 is the target date, we still have three and a half weeks. I'll also get our friends at Scotland Yard to start a full court press to find McKenna."

"West Point," Kurtzman said softly. "Tons of tourists to see the secretary of defense speak at a cadet parade on a beautiful campus filled with granite buildings. It's one of our national treasures, and it's a perfect target for a dirty bomb."

AN OCEAN AWAY from Stony Man Farm, Inspector Tom Wynsten returned from holiday, logged onto his work computer through a secure line connecting him to the Yard and began scrolling through his incoming e-mails. There was one from Gregory McKenna, and the inspector double-clicked on the icon to open it. He read it once, checked the date window on his watch, then reread the message.

Wynsten had been friends with McKenna for almost thirty years, sharing good times and bad, and there had been plenty of both. He had been a trusty confidant and, while he steadfastly opposed McKenna's vigilante activities, after weighing friendship against professional obligations, he had made the decision to look the other way when Scotland Yard investigated the murders of certain IRA members.

He read the e-mail a third time.

"Be thou at peace, my friend," he said softly as he clicked on the macro to initiate a missing person's investigation.

After a week of overcast skies, the sun broke through, painting Dublin's damp streets in vivid colors. The waters of the River Liffey took on the peculiar turquoise hue that lovers walking hand in hand along its quays find so enchanting and white day lilies, drooping from window boxes of shops along the way, filled the morning air with a cloying fragrance of romance.

Maggie Grylie strolled down Grafton Street, enjoying the warmth. Every so often, she caught a glimpse of her reflection in the store windows she was passing and, when she did, she liked what she saw—a young woman, stylishly dressed, carrying the leather purse she had just bought at Sigmas over on Dominick. It was one of the nicest things she had ever owned and, knowing that it cost more than a nurse could earn in a week, made it even nicer. Since linking up with the IRA, Grylie's life had taken a giant turn for the better.

She had spent the night with Lieutenant Colonel William Palmer, a British officer who told her he was working on a classified project with the IRA. He had been involved that night in the hospital when they had asked her to watch over the American woman who had been drugged. From the very start, Grylie had hoped Palmer would take a liking to her.

She was surprised when she ran into him at the little café

where she liked to stop for a pint or two after work, and quite pleased that he'd remembered her from their rather short encounter almost three weeks earlier. They hit it off right away and, later, she'd invited him back to her flat.

She desperately wanted to escape the social class to which she had been born, and the IRA, she thought, could be her road out. And, if that meant sleeping with a few handsome men along the way, where was the harm in that? Determined to make a success of herself, she would do what she had to do. After the pleasure she had given Palmer last night, she thought there might be a lot more than leather purses in her future.

He had left the flat early. Half awake, Grylie had heard sparrows outside her window greeting the new day as Palmer had slipped from her bed with the experienced ease of a veteran of dawn departures. She had hoped for another round of eager sex, but he'd gotten dressed and had left without a word.

PALMER SAW GRYLIE the moment she turned onto Pearse Street, crowded at that time of morning with commuters heading for the DART station. He fell into step half a block behind, his right hand grasping the ivory handle of a black umbrella that swung at his side.

She had been fun to be with the previous night, a curious blend of low-class breeding and hungry ambition. Why not combine a little pleasure with business? She had obviously been taken with the way he'd trusted her, giving her his real name, telling her he was on assignment with the IRA, letting her feel she was part of an inner group.

She was no different from the many hungry women he had known throughout his career.

Palmer kept Grylie in sight as he allowed himself to be

swept along with the flow of pedestrians. She'd said she was planning to visit her parents over in Bedfordshire and, in response to that information, he had come to the station in the wee hours of the morning to check the platform where trains connecting to sea passage departed. It was one of the center tracks, one of the most crowded runs out of Dublin. It was perfect.

Very softly, so as not to draw attention to himself, he began to chant. The familiar words worked their magic, producing a rush of adrenaline to his brain. The power was coming.

He concentrated on the back of the nurse's head, bobbing in and out of view as she was screened and exposed by the crowd. In his mind, he could see the future. Imagining the scene in three dimensions, he watched himself slip through the crowd, draw close and jab her with the tip of his umbrella.

She might at first think she had been stung—bees were in the air outside—and she might turn and see him.

Her initial expression would be one of confusion at finding him there and, then, as the chemical reached her brain, perhaps an instant of realization would flash across her face. She would attempt to cry out, but the nerve agent would do its work quickly, silencing her talented tongue.

They would lock eyes, and he would nod, smile and slowly walk away, fading into the platform crowd the way a tiger faded into the jungle.

The first thing Bolan verified as he approached Lucino's warehouse was the absence of surveillance cameras.

"They don't need them," Brognola had said while studying the recon photos. "No one has the balls to break into one of Lucino's places."

The second thing Bolan confirmed was the presence of Marcus Arnold's Ferrari in the reserved parking space close to the main door, set significantly apart from the other vehicles. Every Wednesday night, the lawyer came to this warehouse to record the week's business. Bolan was sure that Arnold would have the information he wanted.

In the pouch on his web belt, Bolan carried a larger version of the electronic unit Tokaido had given him for his assault on the import company. This module would clamp an umbrella over the entire warehouse, preventing the use of cell phones. Once the unit was turned on and Bolan cut the telephone landlines, it would be as if someone had put a huge glass jar over the building. Lucino's security forces would be isolated and completely incommunicado.

Bolan snipped an opening in the chain-link fence surrounding the parking lot and soundlessly made his approach. Having rehearsed his attack with the use of aerial photographs, he knew exactly where the telephone lines were encased in an aluminum conduit attached to the one-story building about fifteen feet off the ground.

Once he reached the spot where the lines came in, Bolan pulled a mountaineering pistol from his web belt and threaded a thin strand of high-tech cable in a double back loop through two pitons. After firing the first into the side of the building above the telephone connection, he pulled hard on the cable to set the piton's barbed point into the wood siding the way an angler would set his hook in a prize marlin. Once he was sure that the piton would support his weight, he loaded the second one and fired at a spot about four feet to the left of the first.

By tugging the cable taut to form a triangle with the embedded pitons being two points and he the third, Bolan was able to work his way up the side of the building, pulling first with one arm then the other, shrinking the area inside the triangle as he ascended. Close to the conduit, he drew his foot-long combat knife from the scabbard on his right shin.

Before slicing through the aluminum tube with his blade of hardened steel, Bolan withdrew the electronic assembly from his pouch, removed the protective strip of plastic wrap from the sticky strip on the side of the housing and pushed the device onto the wood siding. When the indicator LED began blinking its operating signal, Bolan cut the telephone cable, throwing the entire warehouse into a communications void.

As he rappelled down the side of the building, he reached into his web pouch for the C-4 plastique he carried. The three chunks of C-4 were about the size of golf balls and as pliable as putty. Thrust into the middle of each was a blasting cap with microchip fuse. When Bolan pressed the timer button on the left side of the watch Brognola had given him, it would emit the proper detonation frequency for all three.

After unhooking himself from the piton lines, he paused for a moment to listen. The yard was dark and still. The only sounds reaching his ears were those made by a pack of rats scurrying through the commercial garbage container at the far end of the building.

Satisfied that his presence had not yet been discovered, he ran around the warehouse to the double-width front door, which was an ugly steel slab with four reinforcing metal bands spot-welded equidistantly from top to bottom. It was the building's only entry, apparently, in order to prevent the occurrence of an attack on two fronts.

Reaching the door, Bolan molded his C-4 into wedges that he could press into the seams behind the hinges in order to direct the plastique's force inward. When he was finished, the powerful explosive resembled wads of gray bubble gum with blasting caps protruding about an inch.

Once he was safely behind a concrete road barrier fifteen yards away, which had been erected during the Mafia wars as a deterrent to truck bombs, Bolan pressed the button on his watch. The C-4 detonated with a concussion that blew the door clean off its frame. The metal bands bent outward, as if sprung by a giant can opener, before falling forward like a castle's drawbridge. Through the smoke, men could be seen running for cover behind wooden crates that filled the area immediately inside the warehouse.

Within seconds, there was a response.

Lucino's troops let loose with a barrage of gunfire. A wall of lethal lead came screaming into the night. Slugs from the left side of the warehouse riddled the parked Ferrari. Those from the right impacted into a deserted warehouse at the far end of the parking lot, chipping away pieces of brick and mortar that fell into little piles at the foot of the wall.

By listening to the volley's tempo, Bolan knew his enemy

was armed with mini- and micro-Uzi machine pistols. From the ebbs and swells produced as the gunmen paused to eject spent magazines and reload new ones, Bolan estimated there were about a dozen defenders.

He drew his Desert Eagle and peeked around the edge of the barrier. Through the door opening, he could see the right side of the room where two men were positioned. Bolan knew that all inside were completely blind to his location, and would have no idea how many attackers were concealed in the darkness outside. With discipline and patience, he could turn their ignorance to his advantage.

One of the men inside dashed across the lighted space, and Bolan fired once, hitting him in the chest. The heavy .44 slug lifted him off his feet, opening a gushing wound that trailed blood as he flew backward.

A medley of angry curses accompanied a new salvo, filling Bolan's ears with the sounds of combat. With the randomness of the returning fire telling him that they had not determined where he was, he lowered himself to a prone position and squirmed to the edge of the barrier.

Two men were within his line of sight, crouched behind wooden crates. They were rising above their cover to fire their weapons, exposing their heads for about fifteen seconds before the Uzis consumed the bullets in their magazines and they ducked to reload. As rounds flew above his head, Bolan waited for the moment when both gunmen would be firing.

The opportune instant came, and he fired twice, the deep-throated retorts from his Desert Eagle less than a second apart. His first shot hit the man on the right in the center of his forehead, ripping the top half of his skull away in a messy eruption. Bolan's second round pierced the other man's throat, the force of the hefty slug all but decapitating him as it shattered his spinal column at the base of his neck before exiting in a crimson rush.

Knowing that his shots would indicate the angle of engagement and thus his position, Bolan drew his Beretta 93-R with his other hand, switching the fire selector to 3-round-burst mode. Sprinting in a crouch toward the open door, he watched for defenders trying to switch to the other side of the room in order to bring him under fire.

Two came running into sight, firing their mini-Uzis from waist level. Before the men could determine exactly where he was, Bolan engaged the first with a 3-round burst from his Beretta, the 9 mm parabellum bullets stitching diagonally across his chest. The man was hammered to the rear, arms flailing, his machine pistol clattering on the warehouse floor. The second gunman dived behind a wooden shipping crate a split second before two rounds from the Desert Eagle chewed through the soft pine, ricocheting wildly off the concrete floor beyond.

As Bolan continued his approach, he slid his Eagle back into its hip holster and grabbed the AN-M8 white smoke canister hooked to his web belt. Flipping the pin away with his thumb, he tossed the cylinder through the doorway where it immediately filled the space inside with thick clouds of acrid-smelling white smoke.

Dashing forward under the concealment the plumes afforded, he reached the edge of the door opening where he hugged the building while pulling a dentist's mirror from his shirt pocket. Keeping himself against the building and out of the line of fire, he used the mirror to look around the corner into the warehouse.

Apparently believing their attackers were entrenched in covered positions outside, Lucino's defenders continued firing into the night. A hot round pierced the Ferrari's gas tank, igniting it with a flash of fire.

The methodical retort of a Streetsweeper suddenly sounded above the din, and Bolan searched through the smoke with his mirror for its muzzle-blast.

The shooter was sweeping from left to right across the open space where the door had been, his rate of fire slow and even, giving the cylinder enough time to rotate and lock into place before the next discharge. In the hands of a panicked operator, a Streetsweeper often skipped, creating a dangerous hang fire that had to be cleared manually. This shooter was patient, and he knew what he was doing.

Using the mirror to aim through the thick smoke, Bolan extended his hand into the door opening and trained his Beretta on the Streetsweeper's flash. When he squeezed the trigger, the 3-round burst found its mark and the combat shotgun fell silent.

Etching in his mind where the other flashes had been, Bolan discarded the mirror and pulled an MK3 percussion grenade from his web belt. When the elliptical-shaped bomb containing eight ounces of TNT exploded, combatants within five meters would be exposed to a lethal shock wave. Beyond the kill zone, casualties would include shrapnel wounds, popped eardrums and concussions. It was the perfect weapon for flushing an enemy from a bunker or reinforced terrain.

Bolan yanked the cotter pin and tossed the grenade into the warehouse, pulling himself back against the outside wall where he'd be shielded from the blast.

As he had expected, the room's enclosed space compressed the grenade's power, amplifying the blast into a mind-numbing explosion that shook the outside wall. Three gunmen dropped their weapons as they fell forward into the open, writhing in pain, blood streaming from their ears.

Bolan grabbed his M-67 fragmentation grenade, removed the pin and rolled the apple-shaped explosive across the concrete floor. In the four seconds before the bomb detonated, he drew his Desert Eagle, ejected the magazine and replaced it with a fresh one. He was in the act of jamming a full magazine into his Beretta when the M-67 exploded with a thunderous roar, spewing deadly fragments in all directions.

Bolan charged into the warehouse, his eyes searching for survivors. A gunman staggered out from behind a damaged forklift, and Bolan let loose with a short volley from the Desert Eagle, punching holes the size of a fist into the man's upper torso. He twisted, as if in slow motion, before falling dead, his body draped across the forklift's tines.

As he ran behind the closest shipping crate, Bolan eyed the four corpses in the middle of the open work area, their shattered bodies telling him they had fallen victim to his grenades. In all, there were ten dead, their blood mingling into little pools as it seeped across the concrete floor.

The concussion from the grenades had dissipated most of the smoke from Bolan's M8 and, although the cordite-laced air in the one-story warehouse was hazy, he was able to see all the way to the far wall, where an enclosed office had been built. As he watched, the door flew open.

"Hey! Let's talk!" A voice amplified through a bullhorn sounded through the warehouse.

Bolan shouted back, "We'll send one of our men. Come out with your hands up."

Three men in dark suits exited the office. Bolan recognized the one in the middle as Marcus Arnold, the lawyer who had fingered Judge Champlain's family. Arnold stared at the carnage in the warehouse, his eyes blazing with naked rage.

Bolan began to walk toward them with both handguns drawn, staying close to the shipping crates in case the need arose to take hasty cover.

"Is there anyone else in the office?" he yelled.

The man next to Arnold hesitated a moment too long before answering, "No!"

The single shot from Bolan's Desert Eagle shattered the man's leg and he fell to the ground screaming. To their credit, the lawyer and his other companion remained standing, staring at their attacker with icy eyes.

"Try again!" Bolan shouted.

"Jake!" Arnold yelled.

A micro-Uzi came clattering through the office door, followed by a man dressed in the long-sleeved work shirt and jeans of a warehouse employee. He stepped over the downed body in the doorway, taking the recently vacated spot next to Arnold.

"Whoever you are," the lawyer said through clenched teeth, "you're all dead men."

"You received a shipment of strontium two nights ago," Bolan said.

He saw a flash of recognition in the men's eyes and knew they had the information he was seeking.

"No. You have the wrong guys," the man on the left said as he lunged at Bolan.

The Desert Eagle roared in response with a .44 steel-jacketed slug to the middle of his chest. The force slammed him against the office wall, opening an exit wound a softball could fit into between his shoulder blades. His lifeless body slid slowly to the floor, leaving a scarlet streak the width of a paint roller.

"I want the owners and I want their location," Bolan said.

"I have the manifest in my pocket," Arnold said, lowering his right hand to reach inside his jacket.

"Slowly," Bolan warned, his combat senses on full alert.

Arnold pulled a paper from his inner pocket and thrust it forward at the same instant that the worker who had been last to exit the office twisted his right arm. Bolan heard the quiet click of a forearm derringer release and, without hesitation, he stepped back from Arnold's outstretched hand while firing his Beretta into the gut of the man at the very instant the tiny gun sprang into his palm. He grunted and pitched forward, releasing the derringer as he fell.

Fear blew across Arnold's eyes, and Bolan knew the lawyer had played his last card.

He slipped his Desert Eagle into its hip holster and snatched the manifest from Arnold's hand. Keeping his eyes and the Beretta locked on his prisoner, he stuffed the paper into his pocket, and said, "Just you and me. Tell me what I want and you live."

"They were Irish."

"North or South?"

Arnold hesitated, but Bolan didn't think it was because he was about to lie.

"They said North, but we checked them out in advance. Our men thought they were IRA."

"Names."

"We didn't ask. They paid cash. They had the right information to claim the shipment."

"Where'd they take it?"

"I heard one of them say something about getting there in an hour."

"How many were there?"

"Six. Armed with MP-5s. We let them know they were surrounded."

Bolan stepped back and motioned with his Beretta. "You're coming with me. Don't try anything stupid."

With the compliance that a man displays when he knows that his life could end at any moment, Arnold walked in front of Bolan through the body-strewed warehouse that stank of death. When they reached the opening where the front door had been and Arnold saw the remains of his Ferrari, he lunged at Bolan.

The 9 mm parabellum bullet from Bolan's Beretta entered Arnold's neck at the base of his skull. Eyes wide and unseeing, Arnold teetered for a few seconds before falling flat on his face.

The Executioner holstered his Beretta, stepped over the lawyer's body and walked into the night.

“You don’t even know him,” Katey Adams said, her voice laced with anger.

“Thinking he’s your friend,” Bolan replied, “is your blind spot.”

They were walking down Baggot Street on the way back to their rooms at the Shelbourne Hotel. Their morning had been spent across the Irish Sea in Bedford, a quaint town an hour’s ride north of London, where they had spoken to the late Maggie Grylie’s mother and sister.

There were two days left in July. The President had no intention of succumbing to the terrorists’ demands, and Secretary Foley refused to cancel his trip to West Point, saying, “Letting them control one day opens the door for them to control my life.”

Homeland Security had raised the domestic-alert level to orange. The CIA and FBI were working around the clock trying to discover Cypher’s identity. Hal Brognola was giving the President and his secretary of defense daily briefings in the privacy of the Oval Office. Bolan and Adams had been sent back to Ireland to pull the thread on Grylie’s murder.

“Put your emotions away for a minute and think about this,” Bolan continued, not noticing the hard set to her jaw his words were causing.

"Bear said that either side could benefit from an attack on the United States. But the North gains only if we give in to the terrorists' demands in order to avert their strike. That's not an option the President would ever consider."

He paused to let his words sink in before continuing. "A more probable reaction is that we'd come out shooting at whoever we thought was behind the threat. And the existence of that new message indicates that the terrorists knew all along how we'd react. Logic tells me it's the South trying to frame their enemies in the North."

"You can't use logic with terrorists," Adams countered. "The Order could have prepared that message to plead their case in the event they were forced to go through with the attack. All the physical evidence points to the North."

"And ninety percent of it was spoon-fed to us. McGuinness knows your job in the White House is planning cabinet trips. He also knows you're the CIA's foremost expert on Ireland. The IRA could have used the communiqué and the agent murders to lure you over here so they could drug you and get details on one of your upcoming trips."

"I don't believe that. Bryan is in danger, too. His name is on the hit list along with all those other prominent Catholics."

"None of which have happened."

"Look at the evidence," Adams said heatedly. "Bobbie Reegan—thug for the Orange Order. And whose fingerprints are on that message intended to be released after the attack? McKenna's! How did the IRA orchestrate that?"

They were strolling past St. Stephen's Green, populated at midday with people enjoying the summer sun. Bolan's eyes scanned the expansive park, but he wasn't seeing the small groups on blankets clustered around the duck ponds or the vendors setting up shop for the rally in support of Irish unity scheduled for later that day. As he walked, his mind was sifting through the data, attempting to match actions with motivations. As he had for three weeks, he ended up going in circles.

"The men guarding Oxford's body were wearing Catholic medals. I think Cypher is with the IRA, maybe working undercover in one of the North groups where he could recruit a few pawns like Reegan for a special mission. Lucino's people thought the dirty bomb was shipped to their warehouse by the IRA. Maggie Grylie's sister told us she was involved with someone from the IRA. Just like Reegan in Stuttgart, they've made all the leads dead ends. Grylie was killed because she was a link back to McGuinness, who was at your hotel that night."

"*After* I was drugged," Adams interrupted. "He got there at seven to take me to dinner and convinced security to open my room when I didn't answer his call."

"So he says."

They walked in silence for a few minutes before Bolan said, "I agree that McKenna's prints on the message are a strong link to the North."

Outside the Shelbourne Hotel, the same street musicians who had been there the day Adams had been drugged were performing their inept renditions, their empty guitar case an apt testament to their talent. "Wait," she said, stopping to donate a few euros to the cause of street musicians everywhere.

"Thank you, m'lady," the singer said. "Are you okay now?"

"You remember me from three weeks ago?"

"Of course. How could we forget when you were taken out on a stretcher? That and you being with Mr. McGuinness. We recognized him from the telly when he arrived, but didn't know then that he was with you."

"What time was it when McGuinness arrived?" Bolan asked.

"Oh—" the singer stared into the distance, remembering "—four o'clock or so." He looked to his girlfriend, who nodded her agreement.

"No," Adams said. "I didn't get here until after five. Didn't Mr. McGuinness come just before seven?"

"Surely, no. He and his friend were here well before you. Like I say, we recognized him from the telly. It was close to seven o'clock when we saw him again—with you in the ambulance. That's why we remember you. We were sad someone who gave us a few quid was taken ill. But you're recovered, I see."

Bolan moved abruptly away, leaving Adams to endure the opening bars of what could have been "Misty." When she joined him in the hotel lobby, he said, "The desk clerk remembers the day because of the ambulance. He confirms McGuinness's arrival time. Let's go get him."

"What? You think you can just kidnap him?"

"You bet I do."

"No way. Especially not today. He's scheduled to speak at the rally across the street in St. Stephen's Green."

"After the rally, then. Him being here that day clinches it for me. He and the IRA are behind all this. You'll see."

THE ATMOSPHERE ON ST. STEPHEN'S Green was a cross between a political convention and a county fair. Religious banners hung from buildings decked with the green, white and orange of the republic and strains of Irish music floated on the light breeze. Children selling roasted chestnuts pushed through the crowd, followed by vendors lugging coolers of stout and flavored ice to wash down the mealy nuts. Excitement rippled through the air.

Bolan and Adams walked the three blocks down Grafton Street from their hotel to the green. Once they got to the stone archway opposite Sinnots Pub, the people became so dense they were almost separated by the crowd's ebb and flow.

"This is incredible," Bolan said. "You'd think they were in the middle of a revolution."

"To an Irishman," Adams replied, "this is a revolution. An uprising against the Crown begun by that man." She pointed to a statue of Padriac Pearse immediately outside the black iron fence.

"The Nationalists consider themselves the last British colony, struggling to set Northern Ireland free to join the republic. But Ireland can't survive economically on her own. She must remain part of the UK to compete against NAFTA and the Pacific Rim. Unfortunately, this is also a religious war. There may never be a solution."

The speeches were about to begin, and the crowd displayed its enthusiasm. People clapped, stamped in unison and sang Irish songs. When the first man stepped to the microphone, he looked frightened by the force he could undoubtedly feel pulsating in front of him. He read a short speech condemning violence, condoning peaceful assembly and urging everyone to support the cause.

"What's the story on this guy?" Bolan hollered above the din.

"There's a structured format to these rallies," Adams replied, clearly enjoying the excitement. "The speakers will drive the crowd into a frenzy. If rioting breaks out, the rally committee will point to this introductory speech and say they took a stand against violence. Then they'll argue it must have been British agents in the crowd who caused the trouble. I've seen it dozens of times, especially during Marching Season."

The master of ceremonies stepped forward to introduce the first speaker.

"A native of Dublin," he shouted into the microphone, "one of our own. You know him from his editorials at the *Independent.* A true friend of the republic, a learned man, his pen is mighty, indeed. Let us welcome today this Catholic, this Irishman, this patriot! Ladies and gentlemen, Bryan McGuinness!"

Many in the crowd knew McGuinness personally. Most who did not were familiar with his editorials. They applauded and cheered thunderously as the editor crossed the stage to the microphone.

He was dressed in a black turtleneck sweater and tweed jacket. On his lapel, a small pin bearing the colors of the republic winked in the waning sunlight as he turned to acknowledge the audience.

Standing on the stage overlooking St. Stephen's Green, surrounded by bunting, Bryan McGuinness was the personification of the revolution. It took but one look at the man to know he was Irish, Catholic and well educated. Here was a leader, a modern-day St. Patrick, ready to drive the British from his land.

McGuinness began by addressing the crowd in Gaelic.

"God and Mary be with you." His amplified voice boomed out over the park.

"My brothers and sisters, we stand united."

"Ireland for the Irish!"

The crowd went wild. Their deafening response echoed off the buildings surrounding St. Stephen's Green, reverberating until the very ground shook.

Being an accomplished public speaker, McGuinness knew how to control his audience's emotions. As the cheers died out, he continued in English.

"For many years, our country has been divided by the invading British. If we wish to see our land united, Catholic as it shall be, we must take it upon ourselves to act."

He paused while roars of agreement filled the air.

Lieutenant Colonel William Palmer had an unobstructed view of the rally. The stage was straight ahead. All approaches, save for a tiny area blocked by the giant willows on the west bank of the duck pond, were within his field of fire. He could engage targets across a panoramic span, but he already knew that would not be necessary.

He settled into a comfortable sitting position behind one of the rooftop buttresses. The time was drawing near—not only for this day's major milestone, but for the entire operation. Every night for the past week, he had met with McGuinness to reassure him he knew exactly what to do once he got to West Point to claim their place in history.

He opened the guitar case next to him and slid his hand down the barrel of the Heckler & Koch PSG-1 sniper rifle.

Through it all, Palmer thought, McGuinness had been a genius. Granted, he hadn't come up with the actual assassination plan, but, once Katherine Adams gave them the details of Foley's schedule, killing was the easy part.

And the CIA had played into their hands at every turn. From the initial murders to lure Adams to Ireland, to the way McGuinness misdirected her superiors, the entire operation was admirable. At this very moment, American agents were probably chasing their tails up North, where they'd still be on

August 17 when the evidence against the Orange Order would be stacked so high the CIA would wipe them out exactly as McGuinness predicted.

The rally would seal their fate. McGuinness had told him that the communiqué intended for release after Foley's assassination had already been discovered. His source at Scotland Yard said the CIA was asking about McKenna—proof that they were onto the fingerprints. And, after today, everyone would believe the rumored assassination list was real.

Palmer peeked through the concrete filigree at the park below and began to chant. As the familiar rush of adrenaline flooded his system, he took the sniper rifle from its case, cradling it firmly into his shoulder. For a brief second, while adjusting the telescopic sight, he remembered a violin teacher with whom he had studied during his high-school years.

"Fingers before bow," the old Russian would scold when Palmer tried to play the instrument before being fully set.

"Fingers before bow," he said softly, the phrase bringing a smile to his face as he pressed his cheek into the hardened plastic stock.

He peered through the sight at the crowd, placing the crosshairs on people he recognized, enjoying the thought of their faces exploding if he deemed to pull the trigger. When he came across the two Americans, he stopped short. Adams could be explained, but what the hell was the man from Stuttgart doing here?

He lowered the rifle and sat back. Was it possible they were onto McGuinness? Palmer didn't think so. McGuinness was simply too far ahead of them. But their presence was the second unexpected deviation from a plan that, one month ago, had been flawless. This man's presence in Stuttgart had been the first variation from the planned script. Here was another. There was no reason for them to be at the rally.

Palmer knew he could easily kill them both, two shots in less than three seconds. But a double CIA murder would confuse the message. One might be all right, but definitely not two. Even one was risky. Palmer quickly considered possible outcomes and made his decision.

Planting the meaty portion of his triceps onto his knee, he leaned forward, checking himself for proper alignment—ankles crossed, right elbow tucked into his side, finger resting alongside the trigger. His left hand was supporting the rifle grip, spine slightly curved, his torso was pulled into a compact mass with no bone-to-bone contact.

The two Americans were ten feet from the edge of the stage, watching McGuinness.

Palmer's lips moved rapidly, chanting the words that brought him power. He slowly inhaled, filling his lungs to their limit.

He exhaled.

In again, he held his breath, placed the crosshairs on his target, slid his finger onto the trigger.

Very gently, he squeezed off a round and through the scope, watched the man's head disappear in an explosion of bone chips and blood.

Slowly, he exhaled.

Bolan turned, his mouth open to speak, but the distinctive sound of lead smashing into flesh stopped him short.

Everyone around them froze, staring in shock at the blood-splattered podium where, an instant earlier, Bryan McGuinness had stood. Bolan and Adams fell to their knees and automatically looked in the opposite direction, searching for the round's origin. There had been no sound, and neither of them could locate a trickle of smoke.

"Silencer! Can you see where it came from?" Bolan shouted.

"No!" Adams shouted back while scanning the buildings at the far end of the park.

"Stay down," Bolan ordered.

The crowd recovered quickly from being stunned, and people began to run in all directions. Some tried to push their way to the stage, others dived for shelter and some ran haphazardly, compelled by their fear simply to move.

Bolan stood and shouted above the pandemonium. "Let's get up there before we're trampled!"

He grabbed Adams's hand and, together, they threaded their way through the men and women pressing against them. By the time they got to the stage, police had cordoned off the platform. They displayed their American passports carrying a special seal for law enforcement, and the officers let them through.

McGuinness was lying on his back. Although policemen and paramedics crouched over the body, one glance told Bolan why they were not attempting CPR.

The upper half of the man's head was completely gone, and a river of blood had gushed from the wound onto the platform's wooden planks. Adams knelt close, her face contorting in spasms as if she was about to cry. Bolan put his hand on her shoulder.

"Let's go see Fontes," he said.

Adams stood and nodded, pausing to take a last look at the bloody stage and bunting before following Bolan back into the crowd.

EDMUND FONTES WAS hanging up the telephone when Bolan and Adams entered his office.

"Holy shit! Were you there?"

They nodded.

"Holy shit!" he repeated. "There'll be riots tonight, for sure. I hope to God they don't storm the embassy."

Bolan slid into one of the wooden chairs in front of Fontes's desk.

"Have the police recovered any evidence?" he asked.

"Evidence?" Fontes repeated as he moved behind his desk. "They've got evidence from here to Timbuktu." He pointed to the telephone. "That was one of my men. They have the weapon—Heckler & Koch sniper rifle with telescopic sight, firing 7.62 mm rounds. The shot came from a roof across the street. The rifle was left at the scene."

"Prints?" Bolan asked.

"They have it in their lab, but I doubt there will be. They also found an orange scarf. But that's not all. When you return to your hotel, you'll find I left a message for you to call me. This is why."

He opened his top drawer and withdrew a CD. "Earlier today," he said, "the government responded to a tip and raided a depot near Stormont Castle up north. There was no one to arrest, but the raid yielded the usual—explosives, a few Kalashnikovs and reams of anti-Catholic literature. Also, this CD, which is a copy of the one I passed on to you last week. Same message."

"Do you think August 17 is the date?" Bolan asked.

Fontes nodded grimly. "Yeah. I agree with Brognola's analysis. The Apprentice Boys, Marching Season, Foley's schedule, it all fits for an attack at West Point on the seventeenth."

"But is it the Order? Before the rally, I was convinced it was the IRA," Bolan said.

"McGuinness told us his name was on the assassination list," Adams added.

"Killed, I would think, by the same people who murdered our agents," Fontes said.

Bolan turned to Adams. "Foley will be at West Point on the seventeenth. Where will Moore be? They were the two McGuinness had said were on the list."

Fontes shook his head. "The message on the CD says 'him.' It's not Moore."

Bolan closed his eyes and rubbed his temples. "We don't want to overlook anything. Can we cancel the West Point portion of Foley's trip?"

"No way," Adams replied, "we've already been down that road."

"If the attack is planned for the seventeenth, we have nineteen days to stop them. There may be one assassin, there may be many. But one of them, the one who killed McGuinness, is here tonight. We can get to the States before he does," Bolan said.

He pushed himself out of the chair. "You and I will wait for them at West Point. I don't know how yet, but we'll stop them there. And, the more time we spend at the academy, the better off I think we'll be."

He turned to Fontes. "Thanks for your help."

Fontes stood and shook hands with his visitors.

"Good luck," he said.

“How was he found?” Inspector Wynsten asked.

“Hunters,” the junior investigator named Wilk replied. “Dogs sniffed ’im out, rooted up the body.”

Wynsten resumed sifting through the fingerprint-smudged black-and-white photos. “Jesus. Right in the eye.”

“The CIA is looking for him. His fingerprints showed up in one of their active cases.”

“Give them everything we have,” Wynsten said, without looking up. He stopped and tilted one of the photos toward the light.

“What’s this?” he asked. “The white stuff on his hands.”

“Calcinated gypsum.”

Wynsten reached for the magnifying glass he kept on his desk. “Plaster of paris?” he asked, while viewing the enlarged image.

“Yes, sir. Both hands.”

“Like someone made a mold of them?”

“Yes, sir,” Wilk replied, “that would be one explanation.”

Wynsten thought for a moment, then said, “Let’s keep this quiet. Out of the press, I mean. Get me the name of the American agent asking for information, and I’ll contact him directly. Let’s not tell anyone else.”

Wilk nodded and reached for the photos.

"I'll keep these," Wynsten said, sliding them into their folder.

"YOU'RE A HARD MAN to reach," Wynsten said by way of greeting.

"I apologize for the circuitous route. I'm not exactly assigned to a CIA section, but we're—"

"I know who you are," the inspector interrupted, "and I can surmise the type of section you support. You have a warrant out for a certain vigilante who became known as McKenna."

Hal Brognola's heartbeat quickened. "Yes. Have you found him?"

"We have."

"Do you have him in custody?"

"He's dead."

"Are you sure it's him?" Brognola asked.

"Quite."

"When and how was he killed?"

"Sometime between the eighteenth and twenty-first of July. Stabbed through the eye with a knife."

Brognola jotted the dates onto a pad by his phone and asked, "How confident are you of the dates?"

"Very. I have collaborating evidence I cannot share with you, but I know with one-hundred-percent certainty that he was alive on the eighteenth, and dead on the twenty-fourth. Our forensics experts have been able to back off the end date a few days to the twenty-first."

"Scotland Yard has prints from crime scenes that supposedly were his," Brognola said.

"And, because he was not in our databases," Wynsten picked up the thought where Brognola left off, "we were never able to link them to an actual person. Now we will know who McKenna was."

"Is it possible the prints on file do not match the body? The reason I ask is because I was told this morning that those prints were on the weapon used to murder Bryan McGuinness. Are you familiar with the case?"

"I am," Wynsten answered. "We've had more than a passing interest in McGuinness over the years. It was my laboratory that matched the prints from the murder weapon. I haven't told anyone that McKenna was dead at least a week prior to McGuinness's death."

Before Brognola had a chance to ask why he hadn't, Wynsten continued. "When we found the body, there was plaster of paris residue on both hands. I immediately surmised that McKenna's killer took a mold of his hands in order to plant his fingerprints at other crime scenes. "In cases involving misdirection it's often prudent to play along and see where the perpetrator is steering the investigation. It appears that you, Mr. Brognola, are the one who is being misdirected. You are also the only man outside my group who knows that McKenna is dead. I hope the knowledge will be to your advantage."

"How long can you keep his murder quiet?"

"No more than another week. The actual date of his death, two weeks perhaps."

"Thank you. One last question. Have you been able to reconstruct the killing? What kind of knife, for instance?"

There was a slight rustling over the phone, leading Brognola to assume the inspector was leafing through a case file.

"It was a double-edged blade, quite slender, a throwing knife, we're thinking."

"Do you think that's how McKenna was killed? By a thrown knife? Rather than being stabbed, I mean?"

"We have no way of knowing that," Wynsten replied. "But we have hypothesized that a man possessing McKenna's reputed skills would not be expected to end up on the wrong side of a knife in a hand-to-hand skirmish."

"Who could throw a knife into someone's eye? The only place I've seen skill like that is in a circus."

"Or," Wynsten suggested, "at a dart championship."

As soon as they hung up, Brognola called Aaron Kurtzman at Stony Man Farm.

“The secretary won’t cancel?” Bolan asked Hal Brognola.

“Absolutely not. He nearly took our heads off when Adams and I pressed it with him before coming up here yesterday. He ended up throwing us out.”

They were strolling down Diagonal Walk, glancing in all directions as they progressed from the Plain’s northeast corner by Doubleday Field toward Eisenhower Barracks, where a ten-foot statue of Douglas MacArthur stood on a granite pedestal, his belt buckle the only shiny spot on the weathered bronze. One of the many legends at West Point was that plebes in poor academic standing could appeal to MacArthur’s spirit by keeping his belt buckle spoony.

“Bomb dogs until after he leaves,” Brognola said with a nod directed toward a canine team off to their left.

“When does he get in?”

“Tomorrow evening. We have the superintendent’s reception, then the full schedule with all the activities on Thursday to worry about.”

“It’ll be here,” Bolan said, “during the parade.”

It was midday and heat waves shimmered off the Plain’s flat grassy surface. Small clusters of new cadets receiving marching training under the stern guidance of upperclassmen were assembled at irregular intervals across the parade field, while a trio of drummers from the drill squad maintained a constant beat for the instruction, working in three-man shifts from 0630 to 1700 hours.

Brognola watched as another of the dog teams sniffed around the entrance to the pedestrian tunnel running under Thayer Road.

"They'll sweep through a dozen times each day," he said. "Adams also has Secret Service in Eisenhower Barracks and the superintendent's house watching the Plain around the clock. If he tries to plant the bomb ahead of time, we'll nab him."

"Or her. Let's not ignore anyone," Bolan said.

"Or her," Brognola agreed.

They continued to walk down the paved diagonal path bisecting the Plain, their eyes searching for anything out of the ordinary.

"Inspector Wynsten called me this morning," Brognola said, without breaking stride.

"And?"

"He had the results of two autopsies. The first was Nurse Grylie's. She was injected with VX."

Bolan nodded knowingly. "She could have tied McGuinness to Katey's drugging."

"The second was his. He was in the final stages of inoperable lung cancer. When it gets into the lobes like that, there's nothing you can do. From the level of painkillers in his system, Wynsten says he must have been living in agony."

"McGuinness sacrificed himself to convince us his assassination list was real. If you're dying, anyway," Bolan surmised, "why not put a quick end to it and maybe strike a victory for the republic in the process? Kill our agents to lure Katey over there so she could give them the information they needed. Use Reegan, the communiqué and the assassination list to point us North. Then make us think McKenna is involved so we'll go in and whack the Order. It's a slick plan. No way to prove any of it, though."

"And it's not over yet. The bomb is around here somewhere, waiting for the day after tomorrow."

"Maybe we're facing a dual attack—guns and bombs," Bolan said.

"The barracks building is the closest and, even if he could get past the guards we'll have on duty, that would be one hell of a shot," the big Fed replied.

"It's not as far as when he shot McGuinness."

"Yeah—" Brognola finger-combed his hair and swallowed hard "—but we can control who gets into the barracks."

"I'm not sure we can. What if he's dressed like an officer? Or a cadet?"

"Too old for a cadet."

"A woman could pass for a cadet."

"We'll have to make sure the guards on every floor positively know who's in the building. The roof is safe. Our marksmen will be there."

"Are we sure about the bleachers?" Bolan asked.

"Metal detectors, dogs, portable X-ray scanners. There's no way someone will get a weapon into the bleachers or anywhere close to the reviewing stand."

"So they'll have to find a way to plant the bomb on the Plain."

"In addition to the dogs," Brognola said, "we'll be taking IR photos throughout the day. The only other way is to carry it in and, if he tries that, the scanners at the entrance to the bleachers will catch it."

Instead of responding, Bolan put his hands against the sides of his face like blinders and slowly turned in place, taking in a 360-degree view of the area surrounding the Plain.

"Last year in Colombia," he said while turning, "a trained falcon flew a bomb right into the microphone on a reviewing stand."

"Katey covered that this morning with the Secret Service. We'll have a dozen marksmen with shotguns positioned around the Plain. They'll shoot anything—bird, dog or whatever—that makes a move toward the reviewing stand. Think how slowly even a fast bird flies if you're watching for it. In that regard, it's to our advantage that the Plain is so open. We'll see a bird for a long time before it reaches the secretary."

"What about an unmanned drone? Maybe one with pontoons coming off the Hudson?"

"Swift boats will be on the river, and airspace from Newburgh to New York will be under radar alert. We'll have a squadron of F-16s from Stewart in the air, ready for intercept and, right over there on Doubleday Field, we'll have a fully armed Cobra."

"If you wanted to blend in here," Bolan said, eyeing the cadets marching back and forth in their groups, "you'd wear a uniform."

Brognola nodded. "If anyone in uniform, especially a cadet, rushes toward the secretary, we'd better be ready to take him or her out quickly and ask questions later."

"Take. As in shoot?" Bolan asked.

"God, I hope not, Striker," Brognola answered. "But we'd better be ready."

PALMER GLANCED UP and down the deserted street. Although tourists outnumber residents at West Point by more than fifty to one during the summer, this part of campus was of no interest to visitors.

The plan was progressing well. Computing power had

been the only variable, but Palmer knew West Point had powerful labs and he would not be forced to use his slower laptop and modem.

He checked the little map he had picked up at the welcome center across from the hotel, matching the number stenciled on the brick building in front of him to the legend on the map. Of the three computer labs available, this was the most remote. Tucked into the far corner of Buffalo Soldiers' Field, it was not likely he would be disturbed there.

He entered the building, a converted stable with a doorway low enough to make him duck. Once inside, he saw he had guessed correctly. The layer of dust covering the floor told him that no one had been inside for at least a month, maybe not since May when classes had ended. He walked to the workstation in the far corner, moved the chair and table so he had a view of the door with his back to the wall and turned on the machine.

From his pocket he withdrew a scrap of paper with access codes that he had downloaded from the Cray Supercomputer at Sandhurst. He typed the first command, read the directions on screen and began to walk down the electronic path leading to West Point's computer system.

In less than ten minutes, he understood the security protecting the military academy's mainframe, the protocol for virtual private network dial-ups connected into the system and the procedure to access training files. He studied the main menu, searching for the sophomore curriculum. Before calculating azimuths, trajectories and charges for the guns, he needed to verify the training sites.

Palmer hummed Broadway show tunes as his fingers flew across the keyboard, the cursor on screen dancing from one application to another as if responding to his music.

After slightly more than an hour, he leaned back in the

chair and laced his fingers behind his neck. The task had taken longer than he'd anticipated, but he had finally found the schedules and gun locations.

He watched the screen, smiling at what he saw. The computer was conducting mock firings with a program he had written on the Cray back home. Every possible weather condition was being considered, with the result of each trial plotted on an overlay of the Plain. The Xs indicating where the rounds would fall appeared, one by one, in a tight circle around the reviewing stand. Each was within the kill zone for a high-explosive shell. Initial casualties would come from the detonation, with the aftereffects of the strontium's radiation lasting for months. The attack, he thought, would be devastating to the public psyche.

When the simulation program ended, Palmer ejected the CD and slipped it into his pocket. Although his name would never be known, he was convinced he would go down in history as one of the greatest assassins ever.

HAVING ARRIVED midafternoon, Akira Tokaido joined Katey Adams, Hal Brognola and Mack Bolan for supper that night in the West Point Officers' Club where the maître d' gave them a table with a panoramic view of the Hudson. Below them, not far from where a great chain had been stretched across the river in revolutionary times to prevent the British navy from dividing the colonies, sailboats glided by, creating a scene far different from what Adams remembered from a winter trip she had made to the academy ten years earlier with the MIT pistol team.

"He must have used a Cray," Tokaido was saying, his words pulling Adams from her reverie.

The Stony Man team had compiled a file on McKenna that Tokaido was sharing with the others. "All his messages came through encrypted military channels," he said, tonguing a wad of bubble gum into his cheek. "Crays are the only machines with enough power to crunch the algorithms his sources used. His killer must have had access to one."

Adams was about to say something when they were interrupted by the arrival of a tall man wearing a British army uniform.

"Katey?" he asked.

Adams rose and extended her hand. "William! What are you doing here?"

"Academy exchange," he said, glancing at the others. "And you?"

Adams shook her head and, instead of answering his question, introduced him as Colonel Palmer of the electrical-engineering department at Sandhurst.

"I've read some of your articles in the *Advances in Engineering Education* journal," Tokaido said. "Very cutting edge, especially your modeling work."

"Thank you," Palmer said with a smile. He turned to Adams. "Perhaps you'll join me for a drink after dinner?"

She winced, said, "Sorry, I can't. Not tonight. Maybe another time?"

A cloudy countenance stormed across his features. "Of course," he replied. He paused, and an awkward silence lingered between them. "Well, it was nice seeing you," he said, and, with a quick nod, left to join his dinner party.

"He was one of Bryan's friends," Adams said before anyone had a chance to ask. "I met him a few times when I was in Ireland."

"Do you know him well?" Bolan asked.

"Not very. He's one of the most obnoxious, egotistical men I've ever met. Why?"

"It strikes me as an odd coincidence that one of

McGuinness's friends would be a world-class sharpshooter. You know, considering how he died, I mean. Colonel Palmer is wearing a shooting medal that's awarded to less than one percent of NATO officers."

"If they had a medal for arrogance, he'd be in the top one-thousandth of one percent."

Everyone except Bolan laughed at the wisecrack.

Palmer remained still, observing the cadets. These were not the ones who would be here when his men took control of the site. The cadets scheduled to rotate through to fire the guns were currently on the other side of Camp Buckner, completing their assignment as forward observers. Fate was dealing the young people here a living hand while simultaneously signing death sentences for their classmates.

The man from Stuttgart had been at dinner the previous night with Katey Adams. Palmer hadn't been able to find any information about him. He didn't like his presence there.

But at least their bomb was safe and they still possessed the means to deliver it. And deliver it they would, regardless of whether or not Bryan's charade became exposed. At this point, Palmer was beyond ideologies. The issue at hand was winning, pure and simple. Failure had been an infrequent companion throughout his life. He wasn't about to start accepting defeat now.

The radio crackled, followed by the beginning of a fire mission transmitted from a target range on the other side of the camp.

In the only deviation from combat protocol, the noncommissioned instructor assigned from the 82nd Airborne Division fired a flare gun above the site to signal civilian aircraft wandering into the area that a live-fire exercise was in progress.

Palmer leaned forward, watching every move.

The cadet assigned as battery commander relayed coordinates to his fire control officer who translated them into azimuth and elevation, shouting his calculations to the aimers. This was the third day of gun training, and the ones on the aiming tube, now familiar with the process, twirled the knobs and turned the cranks as if they had been born with lanyards in their hands. The loading team selected the correct number of muslin bags containing the propellant explosive from a wooden box behind their gun, charged the shell by placing the bags into the casing before screwing the warhead onto the shell, opened the breech and jammed the round home with the timely precision of a choreographed performance.

A ballet of death, Palmer thought. He was impressed with the efficiency, notwithstanding his confidence that his own crew would be at least as good.

"Shot over."

The reply "Shot out."

Palmer moved his lips in synch with the transmissions like a teenager singing along with the latest pop hit.

The battery commander dropped his arm, the shooter pulled the lanyard and the woods reverberated with a thunderous echo as the aiming round flew toward its target eleven miles distant.

"Splash over."

There was a pause awaiting reply from the target range, during which it seemed the very trees held their breaths.

"Splash out. Fire for effect, over."

The crews on all five guns leaped into action and were ready within ten seconds to launch a barrage in the shape of a lazy W onto a target far beyond the horizon.

The battery commander raised his arm, sneaking a peek at the British officer who, undoubtedly, was judging the exercise.

King of the Battlefield, Lieutenant Colonel Palmer thought, recalling the field artillery's motto. *Long live the King.*

TOKAIDO AND BOLAN GAZED out the fifth-floor corner window of Eisenhower Barracks. The parade field lay straight ahead, bustling with the added commotion the secretary's trip brought to the Plain's normal activities. To the left was the superintendent's Georgian mansion with its attractive wrought iron veranda. Directly below their window stood the Douglas MacArthur statue on its hefty concrete pedestal.

In its present state, the cadet room they had commandeered would never pass inspection. The wooden doors to the built-in double closets were flung wide-open and the spotless uniforms that were usually arranged in a specified order were shoved to the side to make room for Tokaido's electronic equipment. Wires ran from the weapons rack—which, when the occupant was there would hold either an M-14 rifle or a saber—over the sink and under the bed where they terminated in unauthorized power strips, giving Tokaido three times more outlets than the cadet living there was allowed.

"We don't know how he's bringing it in," Bolan was saying, "but, once it's here, he'll have to detonate it, and I'll bet he won't trust a chemical fuse or a timing device. He'll want control."

Tokaido snapped his gum, and said, "He'll use a transmitter."

"Yes. He'll want it to go off at exactly the right moment."

"Can't do it," Tokaido said, reaching into his shirt pocket for a fresh square of gum.

"You don't even know what I'm going to ask," Bolan said.

While unwrapping the gum, he said, "You want me to jam the Plain to prevent an electronic transmission the way I shut down the cell phones inside that warehouse." He paused, popped the new chew into one side of his mouth while spitting the old one into the wrapper. "Can't do it," Tokaido repeated. "We know the frequency that cell phones operate on. That's why we could jam them. We don't know where on the band the detonation frequency will be. You can't jam the entire band."

Bolan walked to the single bunk, scratching the underside of his chin as he thought. "There's no way you can prevent it?"

"Not unless it's a two-step signal with enough time between the alert and firing sequences for me to see it and then put a jam on."

"It won't be," Bolan said, lowering himself to sit on the narrow bunk. He felt something hard under him. Reaching under the mattress, he withdrew a cadet saber.

In spite of their situation, Tokaido smiled. "You've caught a cadet cutting corners," he said. "I have a cousin who came here. They're supposed to turn those in when they go on leave and check them back out when they return."

Bolan slipped the weapon back under the mattress and lay back, staring at the ceiling.

"We have to stop him from getting the bomb onto the Plain in the first place."

After a slight pause, Tokaido said, "I can't prevent the detonation, but I can record it as it happens. I can map the Plain and, at least, we'll see where the signal came from. Maybe it will help us catch whoever sets it off."

"Yeah," Bolan replied, his frustration evident in his tone, "let's at least do that."

THE SUPERINTENDENT HOSTED a dinner reception at the Officers' Club that evening.

The secretary of defense had arrived on post and security everywhere was tight. At the club's front door, every person was required to pass through metal detectors. All bags, briefcases and purses were searched by a team brought in from Washington.

None of the guests seemed to mind the intrusive measures. Drinking cocktails and chatting with the secretary of defense was a career-enhancing experience the lifers would cherish forever.

A number of cadets were also present, gracefully declining the flutes of champagne offered on trays by roving servers and artfully avoiding the commandant's wife, who had a bit of a reputation for cloakroom indiscretion.

Bolan spotted Hal Brognola in the far corner of the main ballroom by the grand piano and made his way over to him. "Where is he?" he asked.

"Katey has him over at the superintendent's house. He wanted to take a shower and get changed, first. What?"

"Nothing."

Bolan scanned the crowd, picking out the Secret Service agents.

"We're sure we're okay?" he asked. "Him mingling with the guests?"

Brognola nodded without looking his way. "They've all been cleared. Most are senior military, and the bomb squad checked this place less than an hour ago. The kitchen help was handpicked by the superintendent—all waiters with more than twenty years experience in the mess hall."

"Windows?" Bolan motioned toward the French doors looking out over the Hudson.

"Bulletproof glass. We have men outside and the Plain is

under twenty-four-hour surveillance. Unless it's a suicide mission, tonight is okay."

"It won't be a suicide mission," Bolan said. "The parade is the logical—"

Brognola followed Bolan's gaze to Colonel Palmer, who was standing alone by a door leading to the kitchen.

"Something about that guy bothers me," Bolan said. "Let's go see him."

When Palmer saw them approaching, he finished his drink and set the empty glass on one of the little tables draped in black, gray and gold linen tablecloths positioned throughout the ballroom for that purpose.

"Gentlemen," he greeted them.

"Hello again," Brognola said as they shook hands. "Katey told us you were a friend of Bryan McGuinness. My condolences on your loss."

Palmer studied them for a moment before replying, "He was a martyr. Gunned down by Protestant hooligans."

"You say that with certainty," Bolan spoke up, "but the authorities really don't know who shot him."

"Weren't there prints on the rifle?" Palmer asked.

Before Brognola could answer for him, Bolan said, "Inspector Wynsten told us there were partials, but they were too smeared to be of any use. And that makes sense when you think about it. He said it was probably a professional assassin, even though the shot was quite easy. You wouldn't expect a pro to leave identifiable prints."

Palmer fixed Bolan with an icy stare.

"Inspector Wynsten is an idiot," he said, the corner of his mouth suddenly twitching, "and a shot from that distance is anything but easy."

A waiter came through the ballroom striking a chime with

a wooden mallet and guests began moving into the dining room, cutting the conversation with Palmer short.

AFTER DINNER, Brognola and Bolan waited in the Officers' Club bar for Tokaido.

"Here he is," Brognola said, motioning with his head to the doorway where Tokaido stood, peering into the dim lighting. He got up and took a few steps away from their table before the computer hacker saw him and came their way. Brognola sat back down.

"How was your fancy little dinner?" Tokaido asked while pulling a chair out from their table.

"I tried to get you an invite," Brognola said.

"I'm just kidding. Actually, I got a lot done." He leaned forward, and said, "We're all set for tomorrow. Just before the parade, I'll mute everything."

There was an uproar from across the room where a number of officers were playing darts for drinks. Tokaido stretched his neck to look, nudged Brognola and motioned to the game.

"That guy from last night," he said.

Brognola glanced over, then looked at his watch. "We have to get out of here. We still have fifteen minutes, but I don't want to be late if he's ready for us earlier."

They left money on the table to cover their drinks and got up to leave. When they reached the door, there was another cheer from inside, drawing Bolan's attention to the players. He paused in the doorway, riveted in place, until Brognola came back for him.

"Let's go," he said, "I don't want to be late."

"Yeah," Bolan said somewhat distantly. "Yeah. Let's go."

BROGNOLA'S CONCERN about being late turned out to be irrelevant. It was close to eleven o'clock, almost one hour later than they had been told, when the three of them finally got to see the secretary of defense and his chief of staff.

"Mr. Secretary," Brognola said, "I must urge you, once again, to cancel tomorrow's activities. As far as we know, the terrorists are still planning to make an attempt on your life. We firmly believe that tomorrow is the day referenced on that CD."

Daniel Foley nodded understandingly before saying, "Maybe I'll be safe if we cancel tomorrow's activities. Then what do we do? Cancel next week's schedule? Then do I hide for all of next month?"

There was silence.

"Sir, the country can't afford to lose you," Brognola said. "If you can—"

"That's bullshit!" Foley interrupted. "When I was studying government in high school and I saw Johnson replace Kennedy within hours of his assassination, I realized that no one is irreplaceable. Here's the bottom line: No terrorist is going to tell me what I can or cannot do, where I can or cannot go on American soil! Tomorrow I'll be doing my job. I'm counting on you to be doing yours."

There was silence again. Brognola sighed heavily.

"Good night, gentlemen," Foley said. "We have a big day tomorrow."

August 17

The alarm in the guest bedroom went off at 5:30 a.m., and Daniel Foley was immediately awake, instantly alert. He lay in bed thinking for a few seconds before swinging his legs to the side and getting up. Stretching his arms over his head, he walked to the bay windows overlooking the Plain and gazed out across the parade field.

Some great Americans have walked here, he thought, then recalled the words from one of the songs performed at dinner last night by the cadet glee club: *We sons of today salute you.*

A few plebes scampered across the concrete apron in the dim light, completing their morning duties. He considered going out to see them one-on-one, but quickly decided against it. He'd love to do it, to let these future leaders know their secretary of defense cared about them individually, but the security people would go bonkers if he did something like that.

This was the day they were all dreading—the CIA, FBI, pretty much everyone in Homeland Security. Foley was afraid, too, but he wouldn't admit it because there was nothing he could do about it. A person simply could not allow a terrorist to control even one day in his or her life. The bottom line for everyone in the cabinet was that danger came with the job.

Dawn was approaching fast, and he could see the outline of trees around the Plain. If an attack came, they thought it would be during the parade, when he'd be most vulnerable. In his mind's eye, he could see himself lying in a pool of blood next to the reviewing stand. His department would carry on, he was confident of that. His family would be all right, too. They had discussed the dangers around the dining-room table as soon as he received the President's offer. Everyone knew the ground rules from day one.

There was a knock on the door.

"Mr. Secretary?" his aide's voice asked.

"I'm up, Tom," he answered. "I'll be down for breakfast in about half an hour."

His aide's footsteps retreated from the door, and he walked to the attached bathroom to shave.

"YOU'RE SURE THERE'S nothing here."

It was a statement, rather than a question.

"I'm sure," Adams said to Brognola. "The dogs sniffed every inch of the Plain twice already, we have men with metal detectors all over the place and the chopper took infrared photos this morning. There is no bomb here."

"I don't feel good about this," Brognola said. "Is there a better place for a hit?"

Bolan put his hand on Brognola's shoulder. "We're taking the right precautions. The Plain is the logical choice. We'll catch them when they try to bring it in."

"Foley will be in the superintendent's house until eleven. Security there is tight. He'll be driven to the mess hall, and he'll be outside his car on the stairs for less than a minute. That's not a good place to attempt a hit—not with the way it opens right onto the parade field. Inside the mess hall, he'll be safe. After lunch, he'll be driven to the reviewing stand for the parade, and that's the only time he'll be out in the open with crowds around. If an attempt is coming, that's when it'll be," Adams said.

Brognola shook his head while looking at the ground. "I can't shake the awful feeling we've missed something." He walked away, across the grass of the parade ground.

Bolan watched him for a second before moving away from Adams in the other direction. He, too, was deep in thought, trying with all his might to remember every scheme, every plot he had ever heard or read about. How did people smuggle bombs into secure places?

STAFF SERGEANT HECTOR MENDEZ of the 82nd Airborne Division scanned the cadets sprawled on the ground around his field podium. They were at delta gun site, located on the eastern edge of Camp Buckner, and the cadets were about to be placed on alert. For the next six hours, they could expect to receive anywhere from three to twelve fire missions called in from various target ranges surrounding Buckner.

"The battery commander should be at the aiming circle," Mendez said to the twenty-one cadets. "Who's my battery commander here?"

"I am, Sergeant." A tall lanky cadet raised his hand.

"Okay, sir. Go to your position by the aiming circle. When a fire mission comes in, you will use the calculator to determine the azimuth, elevation and charge."

The cadet got up and hustled over to the tripod in the center of the howitzer formation. The five guns were positioned in an elongated W pattern.

"Okay," Mendez said, "when the commander determines the coordinates, he will call them out to the aimers. Where are my aimers?"

Ten cadets raised their hands.

"Aimers set the elevation and azimuth on the guns. Azimuth points the tubes in the right direction, elevation and charge determines range. Aimers, go to your guns."

The cadets rose and jogged in pairs to their assigned howitzers.

Mendez lifted a shell from behind his podium and unscrewed the high-explosive warhead off the end. He held the casing high so the cadets at the guns could see a section of it was hollow, with room to hold up to ten bags of charge.

"Who are the loaders?"

The remaining ten cadets raised their hands.

"Loaders will take one to ten bags from the crate next to each gun, as determined by the calculator."

Mendez took a white muslin bag of charge from the podium shelf and tossed it into the casing. "Each extra bag of charge adds one hundred meters to where the round will land. A good artillery crew will use elevation and charge to put the round exactly where the forward observer wants it. Are there questions?"

There was none.

"Good," Mendez said. "Remember! Do not be afraid to handle these bags. They will not explode if you drop them, step on them or strike them with a blunt object. You cannot set them on fire with a match. They can only be exploded by tracer ammunition, something hot like a flare or the blasting cap that is built into the shell casing."

He turned the shell upside down, allowing the bag of charge to fall onto the ground, and pointed to the strike point on the outside of the empty casing.

He looked at his audience, receiving nods of understanding.

"Okay. After the loaders put the bags of charge into the casing, they will screw the warhead onto the shell and ram the completed round into the gun's breech. Loaders, go to your guns."

The last cadets got up and went to their howitzers.

Mendez surveyed his crews, making sure the cadets were in the proper positions.

"Ladies and gentlemen," he announced, "we are now on alert for a fire mission."

PALMER WAS STANDING behind the granite pedestal of MacArthur's statue when he began his final rehearsal. In his hand, he held an electronic module about the size of a deck of cards. The unit was a transmitter, set to the same frequency as the one carried by his troop commander. This morning, he had verified the coordinates of the gun site and was ready to transmit the proper azimuth, elevation and charge. Having triple-checked the figures, he knew there was no way he would miss.

"Think through the steps," he whispered to himself. "Wait until he's on the reviewing stand and everyone is in place. The gun crew will be ready by then. From here, I'll be close enough to see, but far enough from the radiation."

He glanced behind him to the narrow alleyway running under the mess hall out to the old barracks housing the corps's fourth regiment. Shielded by MacArthur's pedestal when the shell landed, he'd get out of the area with minimal exposure to the strontium.

He smiled, turning the transmitter in his hand.

"It's good," he said out loud.

GAIL BARTON LEANED against the howitzer tube and took a deep breath. Manning the guns was hot, boring work. It was only Thursday, but, already, she was looking forward to the weekend when she could get drunk again. Cadets hid booze up behind tent city, knowing there was no way an officer could get all the way up there without a silent alarm preceding them through the camp.

Glancing across the site at Sergeant Mendez, she fingered the two nips of Jim Beam she had in her pocket. He was telling Iraqi stories to a small group of cadets clustered around the aiming circle who were impressed with him because he had been there. He was impressed with them because they were West Pointers.

She began to walk away from the gun in the general direction of the field latrine, knowing that if a fire mission came in while she was gone, she'd be in trouble.

TOKAIDO STRUCK A FEW KEYS on his computer to bring up the global settings. He was getting a lot of background noise from the scanner, but wanted to wait as long as possible before defining ambient parameters. Once he did, existing noises would be filtered out, causing anything new from the listening wand to be more visible.

He didn't know exactly what the signal from the transmitter would look or sound like, but he knew the less clutter there was, the more chance he'd have to see it. He checked the settings, making sure the recording mode was ready and synched.

Noises from the assembling crowd outside the barracks told him the time was drawing near. The secretary was already inside the mess hall, having lunch with the corps.

He stepped to the window and glanced outside. The Plain glistened in the afternoon sun like a well-tended fairway. Tourists stood along the perimeter, anxious to hear the secretary's words on the war against terrorism.

He could see Bolan and Brognola standing across the Plain next to the reviewing stand, the former dressed in fatigues, wearing the rank of a military police colonel and armed with his Desert Eagle and Beretta 93-R.

Tokaido returned to his monitor, deciding he could begin filtering ambient noise. The parade would start in less than an hour.

KEVIN BURNS PEERED through the thin woods of Camp Buckner, finding the closest members of his commando team. The objective was straight ahead, and he gave the hand signals to initiate their assault. It was unfortunate that innocents would be killed, but the war had been claiming innocents in pubs and train stations throughout Ireland for almost a century. With the righteousness that comes with doing God's work, Burns was willing to kill a few more for the cause.

The commandos inched forward, their MP-5s set on full-auto.

Their attack was brief and brutal. The soldiers had divided the gun site into areas of responsibility ahead of time and, when they emerged from the woods with their weapons chattering a staccato song of death, the cadets were slaughtered like lambs.

Staff Sergeant Mendez managed to fire his flare gun into the air before he was cut down with a burst of 9 mm lead that felled him into the woods at the edge of the underbrush, his custom-made signal pistol gripped in his hand. By the time the flare burned out, the lives of all at the gun site had also been extinguished.

The commandos moved forward and took their positions at the guns, awaiting the fire mission from Colonel Palmer. Burns shouted an order into the woods, and two men came forth lugging a high-explosive artillery shell.

The round's warhead contained 150 curies of radioactive strontium.

INSIDE THE MESS HALL on the main campus, Secretary of Defense Foley turned to the commandant of cadets.

"General," he said, wiping the corner of his mouth with his gold napkin, "this is a beautiful post. I'd like to come back sometime when the entire corps is present."

"You're always welcome, sir," the general replied, glancing at his watch. "We should leave if you're ready. The cadets will be dismissed in five minutes and they'll be in a rush to change uniforms for the parade. If we want to avoid the stampede, we should leave now."

"Fine with me."

They walked down the stairs of the Poop Deck, the little medieval castle at the center of the mess hall where dignitaries dined with a view of all four wings. Upon reaching the bottom of the stairs, they turned down the center aisle, walking past row after row of cadet tables leading to the front exit. As they passed, members of the corps rose and cheered.

When they opened the main door and stepped into the brilliant sunshine, a thunderous roar greeted them. Thousands of citizens from New York, New Jersey and Pennsylvania had come to see the secretary of defense. People stood twelve, maybe fifteen, deep around the entire circumference of the parade field.

Foley stood at the top of the stairs and waved, the crowd acknowledging his gesture with wild applause. Caught in the adulation, he turned to the commandant.

"Forget the limo!" he shouted over the din. "Let's walk across the field. We'll give these fine Americans a chance to see their secretary of defense up close."

Before the commandant could respond, Foley descended the stairs and stepped onto the manicured grass to begin a five-minute walk across the Plain.

ACROSS THE PARADE FIELD, Hal Brognola's earplug crackled, and a voice came through on the frequency being used by Homeland Security.

"This is Jay. What the hell is he doing?"

Jay was the ranking Secret Service agent on the reviewing stand. He could see that the secretary was about to start his walk across the parade field.

"Jay, this is Bob, the driver. He's going to walk."

"All agents, this is Jay. Pete, Turner, Jim and Frank. Get around him now!"

Four men in dark suits emerged from the crowd and surrounded Foley and the commandant.

"Can you believe this? We're on alert for a professional assassin, and the secretary decides to take a stroll out in the open with ten thousand people around. Jesus Christ, I'm getting too old for this." He continued talking into the radio, his eyes glued to the men walking across the Plain. "Okay, we're still good. Everyone, stay sharp."

Bolan was seated in the bleachers off to the far left of the reviewing stand. An Army captain next to him had noticed his earplug and weapons, apparently concluded he was a Washington staffer and had been talking a blue streak about the corps ever since.

"Yes, sir, forty-four hundred strong," the captain boasted. "Best combat leaders in the world. Trained to lead, trained to think, trained to react under pressure."

"I know," Bolan replied, peering across the Plain at the secretary.

How could I get a bomb to him? Bolan thought.

He scanned the crowd, looking for anything out of the ordinary. In the back of his mind, he could hear the captain spouting West Point statistics.

PALMER WAS STANDING in the shadow of the MacArthur statue at the south end of the parade field when his target emerged from the mess hall. They were on schedule. He touched the module in his pocket, never taking his eyes from his prey.

His lips moved as he chanted, feeling the forces of destiny coursing through him. In his mind, he could picture the carnage he was about to cause that would eventually lead to the unification of Ireland. His hand was about to guide history.

He took a few deep breaths and slowly exhaled. It was almost time. The secretary would reach the reviewing stand, and the cadets would march onto the field. Then it would be time for his speech, time for his death.

FROM HER POSITION in a clump of thick ferns, Gail Barton could barely believe what she had witnessed. When one of the commandos had slipped past, less than ten feet from where she was hiding in a thick blueberry bush while sipping her Jim Beam nips, she had thought it was all part of the training exercise. They had moved quickly into the gun site, and, once the attack started, she realized it wasn't blanks they were shooting.

She drained the remainder of the whiskey, hoping it would stop the trembling that was shaking her like a rag doll, and tried to think. Mendez had a flare gun that held six cartridges. Maybe a few quick ones in the air would signal someone to come investigate.

As quickly as the thought came, she discarded it. The commandos would shoot her and the flares might not be seen by anyone. A smarter move would be to go find help.

Barton suddenly realized that the absolute smartest thing to do would be to stay hidden, but, in a way she would never have thought possible, she was compelled into action.

"Shit!" she whispered to herself while edging away from the gun site. "This place sucks."

"Do you know West Point is in the top ten colleges almost every year for the number of Rhodes scholars?" the Army captain asked Bolan.

"Yes."

Bolan wished the guy would shut up. He asked himself for the hundredth time how he could get a bomb onto the parade ground.

The secretary had finally reached his position on the reviewing stand, and the band sounded "Attention" followed immediately by "Adjutants Call." The first cadet formations began marching onto the Plain.

"Yes, sir, best marchers anywhere," the captain continued. "Perfectly in step. You think this is impressive. This is only the plebe class and less than half the upperclassmen. These plebes have been here for just six weeks. You think this is something, come back in a few months when the whole corps is here. Then you'll see something."

"I know."

"I still think they should have brought the yearlings over from Buckner. I mean, all these people here, the secretary of defense, national TV, you'd think they'd want both classes marching. And it's not like they're miles and miles away or anything. But, I guess, training is more important. Instead of being over here making a good impression on the American public, our sophomores are just beyond that mountain there, building bridges, going on patrols and firing howitzers."

Bolan turned and looked the captain in the face. "What did you just say?"

"About what, sir?"

"The training. What did you just say? They fire howitzers?"

"Yes, sir, at targets that are miles away. Cadets call in coordinates from a range on the other side of Buckner and their classmates fire onto the range."

"They use live rounds?"

"Of course they do! HE. High explosive."

The plan came together in a flash for Bolan. The dogs couldn't find a bomb on the Plain because there wasn't one. The X-rays and metal detectors were useless. Even the air coverage was futile. It wasn't a bomb—it was an artillery shell. The terrorists were at the guns!

"What's a howitzer's range?"

"Eleven point three miles, sir."

"Can we call them?"

The captain looked at Bolan like he had two heads. "There are no telephones in combat. No, you can't call them."

Bolan looked quickly at the reviewing stand. He could try to stop the parade, but that wouldn't prevent the terrorists from firing the shell and killing hundreds of spectators. He could say to hell with the civilians and try to save the secretary, but Foley would resist and might end up getting killed, anyway.

The only option was to get to the guns before they fired.

"Do you know where they are?"

"The guns? Sure do, sir."

"Let's go. I'm with the CIA."

Bolan grabbed the front of the captain's shirt and pulled him from the bleachers. It took a few minutes for them to wade through the crowd, but then they broke free and were running across Doubleday Field to the chopper. Bolan flashed his CIA badge as he ripped open the passenger door, and the pilot immediately started revving the engine.

"Where to, sir?" he shouted over the whine of the blades.

"Camp Buckner. The gun site."

The pilot shook his head. "Got coordinates? Buckner's a big place. Arty guns, right?"

The captain leaned over the front seat and shouted between them. "I know where they are this week. Fly straight out over the superintendent's house. We'll get there in about four minutes."

The chopper lifted off, and Bolan watched the figures on the parade field shrink.

"Tell me what happens at the guns," he shouted to the captain, who gave him a quick explanation of the field artillery training.

They had been in the air for about a minute and a half when Bolan took the microphone from the dashboard. "I'm calling down to the reviewing stand," he said to the pilot. "What's your call sign?"

TOKAIDO WAS WATCHING his monitor when he saw the transmission spike that he immediately thought was a detonation signal. He jumped, expecting the sound of an explosion.

Instead, a voice came over his computer speakers. "Thunder Forty-niner, this is Eyesight Seven, over."

"What the hell?" he asked out loud, a second before he hit the hot key jamming the entire band carrying the message.

BEFORE THE PILOT HAD a chance to give Bolan his call sign, the radio sputtered and crackled.

"Thunder Forty-niner, this is Eyesight Seven, over."

An irritating electronic buzz filled the cockpit and the radio went silent.

The pilot grabbed the microphone from Bolan's hand.

"Thunder Forty-niner, this is Cobra One. This is an emergency. Please acknowledge, over."

There was no reply.

"There's some type of jam on, sir," the pilot shouted to Bolan. "There's nothing getting through. We're completely blocked."

Bolan looked out the window at the trees while he checked his weapons.

AT THE DELTA GUN SITE, Kevin Burns held the microphone to his mouth.

"Eyesight Seven, this is Thunder Forty-niner, over?" he repeated.

There was something wrong with the radio. His eyes scanned the clearing, from the seven commandos positioned as perimeter security with weapons at the ready, to the three-man gun crew who stood at the center howitzer, awaiting instructions. Without the settings from Cypher, they couldn't fire their shell.

He pressed the transmission button on the side of the microphone. "Eyesight Seven, this is Thunder Forty-niner, over?"

Where was Cypher?

Burns was in a dilemma. Should he fire the shell in the general direction of the academy, hoping to hit something strategic? A total miss, with the warhead impacting in the woods somewhere would be worse than doing nothing. Having a dirty bomb and wasting it would mark them as complete incompetents. They'd be laughingstocks.

Where the hell was Cypher?

Burns noticed the sound of a distant chopper coming their way. He dropped the microphone to the ground and began to shout orders to his troops.

THE COBRA HELICOPTER CAME under fire as soon as the artillery site loomed into view.

"Incoming!" the pilot yelled while banking the chopper to turn her armor-reinforced belly to the attackers as 9 mm rounds struck the motor housing and rear fuselage. The helicopter began to shimmy.

"We're hit!"

Reaching forward to the dashboard, the aviator flipped up two red metal covers, exposing trigger switches for the AMRAM missiles mounted on both sides of the aircraft. As he nudged the stick to turn his ship into firing position, a fresh barrage of parabellum rounds caused him to pull back while launching his hardware. The AMRAMs impacted within seconds, sending two craters' worth of dirt fifty feet into the air with thunderous explosions that echoed across the New York landscape. The Cobra's rotor began to shriek, indicating that one of the blades had been clipped by a bullet.

"We're going down," he yelled as another volley peppered the front of his chopper. A dozen rounds pierced the fuselage below the windshield, zipping within inches of Bolan's face.

The Army captain grunted and fell backward into the sling chair behind the pilot, holding his side where a bloodstain was spreading across his shirt and onto his crisply pressed trousers.

"Flesh wound." He winced as he pushed his hands against his side in an effort to stop the flow.

The Cobra whizzed over the gun site as the tops of distant maples and pines rushed up to grab her. The pilot pulled hard on the stick, trying to point the nose skyward, but the crash was rough in spite of his positioning. He and Bolan were thrown into the windshield when the chopper smashed into the trees, the rotor blades breaking on impact. The injured ship crashed through a number of branches, caught purchase for a moment, then slipped again into a ten-foot drop, coming to a precarious resting perch fifty feet off the ground in the middle of a thick pine.

Bolan pushed himself away from the windshield, tasting blood. Squirming into the area behind his seat, he threw the side door open and grabbed a rappelling rope.

"Get out of the ship!" he yelled as he tossed the rope out the opening.

The pilot was unconscious, and bleeding heavily from his nose and mouth. Bolan seized him by the shoulders as the wounded captain lowered himself onto the floor, grabbed the rope and wound both his legs around it. As he slid out of the opening, Bolan pulled the pilot toward him, hefting his limp body into a fireman's carry.

Wrapping his free arm and legs around the rope, Bolan slid toward the ground behind the captain, carrying the injured pilot across his shoulders. When his feet touched the ground, he lowered the airman and said to the captain, "Stay here with him. Rescue will come to the crash. Are you okay?"

The captain nodded weakly. Clutching his side, he sat on the ground next to the pilot. "It's not fatal," he said. "Good luck."

Bolan drew his Desert Eagle and set off toward the gun site, which he figured was about half a mile away.

As the Executioner ran through the woods, he evaluated the situation. He was sure that his analysis at the parade ground had been correct. The beginning of the fire mission he had heard in the chopper was intended to deliver the dirty bomb. Tokaido had to have been scanning, saw what the frequency was and shut down the entire band before the coordinates could be transmitted. The reason Cypher's plan needed infantry troops was to take over the gun site. They were the ones who had just engaged the chopper.

With all the pieces falling into place, Bolan's primary mission became clear. He had to neutralize the force at the gun site and secure the dirty bomb. After that, he'd work with

Brognola and Adams back at the academy to see what they could do to find the person who had tried to call in the fire mission. He wasn't optimistic about making progress there—that terrorist was probably long gone by now.

He caught movement from the corner of his eye and dropped to one knee, his Desert Eagle at the ready. It was a soldier, running from the direction of the gun site.

"Halt!" Bolan shouted. The soldier slowed, turned his way and came forward with arms held high.

"I need help," she said.

Upon seeing her uniform, Bolan realized she was a cadet.

"The others are all dead!" she said, coming to him. Her knees folded and she went down next to him, where she sat with her face in her hands.

"They came in with machine guns and shot everyone!" she said through her fingers. She was trembling with an intensity that made her teeth chatter.

Bolan put his hand on her shoulder to calm her.

"How many?"

"Oh." She looked up, ran her tongue over dry lips and said, "Seven or eight. No. More than that. Less than fifteen."

"Okay. What weapons did they have?"

"MP-5s," she said immediately. "The kind SEALs use."

Bolan pointed behind him. "Go this way. Our chopper crashed and the pilot and an officer are injured. Stay with them. Help should be there soon."

"I was going to fire Sergeant Mendez's flare gun, you know? I knew it held six flares, and I thought I could signal someone, but—" She stared into the distance as her voice tapered off.

"You did good," Bolan said. "Now, go."

He set off running in the direction from which she had

come, feeling the rush of adrenaline that preceded entry into a hot zone.

The Executioner was on full combat alert and ready to give as good as he got.

Delta gun site was set up in a clearing roughly a hundred yards in diameter surrounded by scrub pines, thick berry bushes and young maples. A dirt trail on the north side of the site provided access for the deuce and a halfs that trailed the howitzers in from the other three firing locations at Camp Buckner and was also the means for the mess hall to bring a hot meal every Friday to the cadets finishing their last day of artillery training.

Crawling through the bushes growing along the perimeter's west side, Bolan came upon the clearing within yards of Sergeant Mendez's body. The corpse had fallen ten feet into the underbrush where it lay faceup, arms fully extended to the sides, flare gun clasped in the dead sergeant's right hand.

As he surveyed the site, Bolan inched toward the body. The flare gun was a custom-designed model similar to the specialty items many field artillery soldiers had used in Vietnam. Mendez's was styled to look like an old-fashioned six-shooter, the cylinder having been retooled to accept signal flares twice as large as shotgun shells. In order to maintain the proper proportions of a Wild West weapon, the barrel and stock were larger than normal, resulting in a handgun bulkier than Bolan's Desert Eagle.

When he reached Mendez, Bolan lifted the flare gun and turned his attention to the site.

Despite having come under fire from the helicopter, the commander had made the decision to deploy his men at the guns, apparently believing a fire mission was forthcoming. Two men stood at each of the five howitzers, each soldier armed with an MP-5 submachine gun. Directly behind each gun was a wooden crate containing the muslin bags of propellant explosive the soldiers would use to charge their rounds. To the left of the formation, the man Bolan assumed to be the leader was talking into a field radio, spinning its frequency dials after every few seconds. In close proximity to the guns were the bodies of two-dozen cadets, strewed about the site in grotesque death poses.

Seeing men at every howitzer, Bolan realized that multiple shells were planned for the attack. He scanned the area directly behind the breech of each gun, looking for the warheads and casings. Once the awaited fire mission provided the team with azimuth, elevation and charge data, the men would marry the warheads, casings and charges into a lethal payload.

One shell—the one behind the middle gun that would normally fire the aiming round—was different from the others. The warhead was slightly larger and appeared to be composed of a different metal than the other five.

From his concealed position, Bolan considered his options. One was to wait and do nothing. Even with the helicopter pilot's inability to broadcast a mayday before going down, help would soon arrive on site. The question was whether or not reinforcements would reach them before this eleven-man fire team went into action.

The forward observer who initiated the fire mission would have switched radio transmission by now to secondary channels, testing prearranged stops along the entire shortwave band until reaching a frequency outside the jam. That was obviously the strategy the leader was employing as he transmitted a message, waited for a reply, then tried again on another channel.

As he watched, Bolan wondered if the unit may have been issued orders to try for a specified period of time before simply firing their rounds into West Point, knowing a hit anywhere on campus would produce the public outrage McGuinness had been seeking.

The Executioner studied the area, registering the positions of the ten armed men. He saw the bodies of more than twenty fine young people who would never have a chance to serve their country. The five warheads were waiting on the ground between the guns and the wooden boxes of charge to deliver the next punch in the war that terrorists around the globe were waging against civilized humanity. He made his decision.

Edging behind the closest tree for cover from the 9 mm rounds that would soon be coming his way, Bolan checked the chambers of Mendez's hefty gun, verifying that it was loaded with five flares. The need to neutralize the howitzers took top priority in his mind as he settled himself with his Desert Eagle in one hand, the flare gun in the other.

After a deep breath to steady himself, Bolan aimed Mendez's six-shooter at the charge box behind the middle gun where the discolored shell sat. When he squeezed the trigger, part of his subconscious mind was praying that the flare's combustive material would burn at a sufficient temperature to ignite the propellant that was designed to be detonated by a blasting cap embedded in a warhead's shell.

Bolan's flare impacted the side of the charge box, easily penetrating the flimsy wood. Without waiting for the result, he shifted fire to the guns on both sides, working his way out from the center of the battery's W configuration. He was engaging the third box when the first exploded with a thunderous roar that sent wood splinters fifty feet into the air. The gunmen scurried for cover behind their howitzers as the second, then the third boxes detonated.

Thick, white smoke filled the air, and the acrid smell of cordite burned his nostrils as Bolan was driven flat against the ground, the space around him suddenly alive with the angry buzzing of deadly lead. The diminished visibility caused by the smoke put someone with Bolan's combat experience at a distinct advantage, and he moved quickly to press the opportunity to its full extent.

Knowing what he would do if he was the one being attacked, Bolan sprinted into the woods away from the clearing. As he'd expected, the three men from the distant gun came quickly, focused on the area from which the flares had originated. Bolan let them pass between himself and the clearing before he opened fire with his Desert Eagle, engaging them individually, as if they were targets in a shooting arcade.

Caught off guard by Bolan's unexpected move away from the objective, the soldiers fell prey to the element of surprise that determined an ambush's success.

The first of the Executioner's rounds slammed into the point man. As the chest wound vomited a torrent of blood, the enemy gunner collapsed to the ground in a messy heap.

Without wasting a second, Bolan shifted his aim to the other two as they turned, almost in slow motion, their minds failing to fully grasp their attacker's true location. The Desert Eagle roared double death within milliseconds. Bolan's .44-caliber magnum rounds hit the soldiers midbody, casting them violently into the underbrush.

The action brought a hail of bullets from the clearing, and

Bolan dived to the ground where the gentle undulations of the New York landscape gave him cover.

With his finger on the trigger of his Desert Eagle, he crawled for a few seconds, then raised himself into a crouch to prepare for a sprint that would take him to a three-foot-high outcropping about ten yards away. Two soldiers charged through the haze that was seeping into the trees, their MP-5s spitting death within inches of Bolan's head before he made them pay the ultimate price. As he dashed toward the rocks, the track of his bullets changed trajectory with his progress, stitching a line, first across the lead soldier's torso, then into his partner's chest.

Muzzle-blasts from two soldiers at the closest gun winked through the fog, and Bolan answered with rapid retorts, his Desert Eagle sounding loud and heavy against the chatter of automatic fire as the smoke from the explosions began to thin.

The outside howitzer became visible and, while firing the remainder of the ammo in his Desert Eagle with his left hand, Bolan took aim with the flare gun, hitting the fourth charge box as bullets cut through the air, causing him to duck below the protective outcropping. His firing pin closed into an empty chamber.

Staying low behind his cover, Bolan ejected the spent magazine with his thumb while grabbing a full cartridge and ramming it into place with the hand holding Mendez's flare gun.

The fourth explosion, with its flash and cloud of smoke, gave him the concealment to change position, and he dashed for the hollow of a berm lining the access road. Rounds struck the rocks in front of him as he departed, their impact sending sparks and chips of granite flying.

Bolan's maneuver placed him at the far end of the battery's

deployment, with four howitzers between him and the remaining charge box. Realizing he was too far away to attempt a hit with his final flare, Bolan reasoned that, in the absence of the soldiers who had attempted the flanking movement, the last howitzer no longer represented a viable threat. Thus reassured, he took aim at the soldiers crouched behind the closest gun's splayed legs.

With rounds snapping past, the thought occurred to him that an errant shot might strike the dirty bomb exactly right to detonate the warhead. As if he had read Bolan's mind, one of the remaining six soldiers, with an obviously suicidal bent, turned his weapon toward the center howitzer and began to fire wildly. His comrades in the immediate vicinity responded in panic, cutting him almost in two with a hail of bullets that jerked and twisted his tattered body like a hooked fish being pulled from the water. As the confused soldiers engaged their perceived traitor, Bolan lay the flare gun onto the ground so he could draw his Beretta 93-R from its shoulder holster.

Rising with coiled spring speed, Bolan raced across the access road to the other side, firing his weapons with both hands. With the 93-R set for 3-round autofire, quick bursts from the high-performance Beretta punctuated the stutter of the MP-5s and the steady bass voice of the Desert Eagle. His changing position opened new lanes of fire, allowing him to pick off the soldiers as he ran across the narrow trail.

The haze from the fourth explosion had almost dissipated as he drew the two soldiers at the closest gun into his line of fire, dealing one a load of .44 lead from the Desert Eagle, the other a serving of 9 mm parabellum bullets. The ammo from both weapons found their targets simultaneously, shoving the soldiers into the artillery pieces that held their already dead bodies erect for a few moments before allowing them to crumple to the earth.

Bolan realized he was down to a final trio who were behind the middle gun, ten yards from the dirty bomb. Charging toward the cover of the first howitzer vacated by the two he had just shot, he was thumped to the ground by a 9 mm slug that caught him in the front of his left thigh when he was still five feet from his destination. Rolling onto his side, he fired both weapons as fast as he could pull the triggers while he squirmed and kicked frantically with his good leg to propel himself forward.

After what seemed to be an eternity of anticipating the impact of a subsequent bullet, he reached a spot behind the first gun where he found protection from fire. After loading his weapons with fresh magazines, he pulled a length of cord from his web belt and looped it around his thigh in a primitive tourniquet.

Although he had been rendered immobile, his new position afforded an unobstructed view of both the dirty bomb and the distant gun with its intact box of charges.

There was a lull in the firefight, allowing Bolan to realize his ears were ringing and he was very close to passing out. He touched his hamstring, coming away with a soaked hand. Even with the cord, his wound was bleeding profusely.

"Hey!" one of the soldiers called out, "let's talk."

Bolan watched in silence from his protected position. One of the soldiers inched away from the howitzer, taking three or four baby steps toward the dirty bomb before Bolan stopped his forward motion with a 3-round burst. The man toppled back like a felled tree.

The remaining two opened fire, their bullets snapping and screaming in flight past Bolan, who remained behind the protection of the howitzer's heavy steel legs. Their barrage came to an abrupt halt while they reloaded.

Bolan waited, knowing that reinforcements would arrive

momentarily. The impasse grew long as an uneasy silence settled over the clearing while the stink of death permeated every nook and cranny within the gun site.

A voice, amplified through a bullhorn, came from the woods, commanding, "Leave your weapons behind and step into the clearing, away from the howitzers!"

As Bolan watched, the two soldiers did as they were told, and the site was suddenly swarming with MPs. The two surviving terrorists were quickly taken into custody and Hal Brognola appeared at Bolan's side, yelling for a medic.

"Are you sure you don't want to spend the night in the hospital?" Adams asked.

"I'm sure."

They were back in the fifth-floor room at Eisenhower Barracks where, earlier that day, Tokaido had initiated the jam that had prevented Palmer from transmitting his fire mission. The room was strewed with electronic equipment, which they had decided to leave until the next day to pack up.

Brognola was listening through earphones to the recording Tokaido had caught of the fire mission's opening call.

"I can't believe Scotland Yard matched his voiceprint so quickly," he said, removing the earphones and laying them on the absent cadet's desk.

"Music photo video files," Tokaido answered while snapping his gum. "Five seconds to e-mail a voice sample over to Europe, the Yard's computer chugs through a million comparisons and, within an hour, you get a match as reliable as fingerprints. Welcome to the digital age."

"An officer from Sandhurst," Adams said, shaking her head. "A perfect cover for an assassin. On academic exchange with West Point, he could have gone anywhere in the States. They picked this trip because it was so easy for them. In addition to everything else, the artillery training at Buckner gave them an ideal delivery mechanism."

"You're right about him being able to go anywhere," Brognola said in response. "Homeland Security will have a hard time finding him."

"He used the Cray at Sandhurst to break McKenna's encryption codes," Tokaido said with a noticeable trace of admiration in his voice.

Bolan lowered himself to the cadet's bunk, and replied in a weary voice, "We should have seen the clues. I knew he was a marksman and, last night, when we were leaving the Officers' Club, it should have registered with us that he was putting on a darts demonstration in the bar. Wynsten told us..." His voice began to taper off for an instant. "A dart champion could have thrown that knife into McKenna's eye."

"He's so brazen! He just can't resist beating others, no matter what. He actually got angry when you said the shot that killed Bryan was easy. It must be eating him alive that he failed," Adams said.

"Striker, are you okay?" Brognola asked.

Bolan nodded while shifting his bandaged leg into a comfortable position in the narrow bunk.

"Yeah. They gave me something in the hospital when they stitched this up. I'll be okay tomorrow."

"We should get out of here and let you sleep. I'll be upstairs in 602."

"I'm three down the hall," Tokaido said.

Adams grinned. "Hotel Thayer for me. White House staff has its privileges."

They said their good-nights and departed, leaving Bolan to drift into a soothing sleep, aided by the sedatives the Army doctors at the West Point hospital had given him.

IT WAS THE SUDDEN WEIGHT on his chest that awakened him.

The August moon shining through the tall windows was bright enough to cast shadows throughout the room. In the silvery light, Bolan could see the wide-open closet doors with the cadet's uniforms pushed to one side; the weapons rack at the foot of the bed draped with wires and electronic equipment; the tiny sink in the corner by the door; and the smiling face of William Palmer, who was straddling his chest, his knees planted on both sides of Bolan's torso.

"A most worthy adversary," Palmer said softly. "Worthy, indeed. Please believe it's an honor for me to kill you this way."

He placed his hands on Bolan's throat to prevent him from calling out and began to apply pressure, slowly and steadily, as if wishing to prolong the power he held over his victim. Weakened by the sedative from the hospital, Bolan swung his arms, feeling a horrible darkness rushing up from the back of his skull.

He struggled to breathe, choking as Palmer tightened his grip.

Bolan's hands groped wildly at his killer's back, grabbing for a finger hold to disrupt his balance. Stars started to explode behind his eyes, and he tried bucking upward, but Palmer was leaning forward, pushing his entire weight into Bolan's throat. With his elbows locked, Palmer's bulk leveraged him into a rock-solid position.

As his fists flailed spastically to both sides, Bolan's right hand slipped into the space under the cadet's mattress where he felt cold metal.

Had the sword been an inch longer, he may not have been able to withdraw the blade from its hiding place and leverage it into the right angle for penetration, but the cadet saber was short enough for Bolan to pull it out from under the mattress and hold it for an instant along his outstretched forearm before thrusting it into a spot halfway between his attacker's armpit and waist.

Palmer stiffened for a second as if an electric shock was coursing through his body before grunting a long, shuddering exhale.

Bolan sucked in a mouthful of sweet oxygen at the sudden relief of pressure on his throat and rammed the cadet's saber to the hilt, causing its tip to exit through Palmer's neck.

In the silvery moonlight, Bolan could see the expression of utter disbelief that crossed Palmer's face an instant before his severed jugular vein doused Bolan with a torrent of hot blood. With his lips moving as if he was chanting, he toppled off the narrow bunk, onto the floor, creating a stain that would take the occupying cadet weeks to remove.

Epilogue

It was a sunny day in Sudbury, Massachusetts, one of the few remaining before late autumn took its turn into early winter.

From the cemetery, they could see Sandy Burr Golf Course, with its fairways and greens in the top-notch condition that grass in New England achieved following the late summer rains, when temperatures had turned cool again.

"He was a golfer?" Adams asked.

Bolan nodded. "I guess so. A guy he worked with told me he drove the ball four hundred yards once when they were in San Diego." He paused. "He was a hero. The intelligence he'd gathered gave us the first crack in the terrorist plot. Without Oxford, McGuinness would have led us down the wrong path."

Bolan let his eyes sweep out over the vista encompassing the golf course and the rolling hills beyond. It was a peaceful scene, seemingly worlds away from the threat of terrorism.

But 9/11 had changed everything, demonstrating to terrorist groups around the globe that they could shift the fulcrum of world power with their cowardly attacks on innocents.

This time, the villains had been stopped, but Bolan knew there was a hate factory somewhere in the world cranking out the next threat, the next terrorist group that would create a hot zone for him to neutralize.

He lived these days for the times between those hot zones, when he could relate as a human being to others and convince himself that there was a purpose for treading the hellfire trail, and that purpose was found in the solace and peace people could give to one another.

Bolan let Adams take his hand as they walked away from Special Agent Oxford's headstone. For the time being, the fulcrum had been reset.

Today, the Executioner would rest, but he would remain alert. Alert and ready to answer his country's next call to duty.